STARS
GO
BLUE

STARS GO BLUE

a novel

LAURA PRITCHETT

COUNTERPOINT | BERKELEY, CALIFORNIA

Library of Congress Cataloging-in-Publication Data

Pritchett, Laura, 1971-
Stars go blue : a novel / Laura Pritchett.
ISBN 978-1-61902-308-6 (hardback)

1. Married people—Fiction. 2. Alzheimer's disease—Patients—Fiction.
3. Caregivers—Mental health—Fiction. 4. Family violence—Fiction.
5. Domestic fiction. I. Title.
PS3616.R58S83 2014
811'.6--dc23
2013044913

ISBN 978-1-61902-308-6

Cover design by Debbie Berne
Interior Design by Neuwirth & Associates

Counterpoint
1919 Fifth Street
Berkeley, CA 94710
www.counterpointpress.com

Printed in the United States of America
Distributed by Publishers Group West

10 9 8 7 6 5 4 3 2 1

Dedicated to
James and Rose
and
Jacob James and Eliana Rose

I.

"I fear I am not in my perfect mind.
Methinks I should know you and know this man;
yet, I am doubtful; for I am mainly ignorant
what place this is."

—WILLIAM SHAKESPEARE

King Lear (act 4, scene 7)

BEN

The fields are poured ice, rippled and waved as if a frozen lake. Ben considers the way the sun has melted—and the earth absorbed—the snow that fell months ago, which is how such strange patterns got created. But he also entertains the idea that his pastures have reverted in time to the great sea they once were. Ben has been partial to water, always, which is why life gets measured in terms of irrigation and rainfall and acre-feet and even the dry rainless days needed for baling hay. Even now he considers the watersheds in his brain, how water moves through tissue, how rivers of electricity pulse in stops and starts.

The pastures have never been this way, so icy, and it makes walking hard. There are no cattle to check, no fields to irrigate, nothing to doctor or wean or birth, and yet he wants to walk anyway, down the iced-over dirt road to the back of his ranch even though the walking is tough because this year the snow has not melted as it should. He has that memory thing—he can't remember the name—and he knows it's normal to be able to remember his childhood but not yesterday and not, on occasion, his wife's name. Or the name of this daughter walking beside him.

He's not supposed to feel bad about the things he can't remember, although he is allowed to feel bad about the fact that this disease only gets worse. Deeper still, he has clarified that he's allowed the terror and the claustrophobia of wanting to say words that are dammed up inside.

She comes more often now, this daughter, she says to walk her dog, a huge yellow puppy that is supposed to bring you things but does not. Just like his brain, this dog doesn't work right. The dog (whose name he can't remember but it reminds him of music) is chasing those big birds out in the field. The dog sends them honking into the sky, and this also reminds him of music. He used to shoot those birds, and his wife would complain because cooking hamburger from one of their cows was always easier than cooking one of those big birds.

He's never seen the likes of a winter like this.

His daughter calls her yellow dog and the creature comes galumphing or galloping or grazing toward them but stops short to pick up a piece of frozen horse manure. "Damn it," his daughter says. "No, Satchmo! No!" She pries the frozen square of manure from the dog's teeth and flings it away. Then she unzips her jacket and sighs one of those frustrated sighs that is supposed to help get patience back and which he hears from his wife all the time now. "Remember, Dad, how you used to say 'tell ya what I'm gonna do, see'?"

Sometimes his brain works if he can manage it like music, like a song, like a river that does not halt. So he singsongs it: *"Tell you what I'm gonna do, see."* With the accent, like a Brooklyn boxer, although he has been a Colorado rancher all his life. He puts up his hands in boxer pose and that makes her laugh and her laugh is like music.

He wonders if she notices how all the wooden fence posts each have a small cap of frozen snow at the top. They put many of these posts in together—he with the posthole diggers and she with the tamping bar—he remembers how proud he was that she could and wanted to do such work. Some of the older posts, the original ones—which are not posts so much as chunks of wood from fallen trees and covered with lichen—are rotting. He tells himself to remember to replace them in the spring. Only he will not be here in the spring.

"And remember how Rachel would say, 'Tell you what *I'm* gonna do, see,' and punch you in the arm."

"Oh, yes. Rachel." He rubs his arm, over the duct tape on his down jacket, where his daughter used to punch him. He has two daughters and one is dead. He remembers her as a child sitting on his lap, twirling her dark fine hair in her finger, and he remembers that she loved to be carried to bed on his back.

"I wonder how my cabin is," he says.

"You just asked me that, Dad. It's the same. It's always the same."

He wonders if it's true, that he just asked that, or that it's always the same. He misses the cabin. He knows nothing about it was ever the same, including the view from the window where the light would change as it shifted across the snowy seas of hayfields, where the small irrigation ditches would sparkle like rows of starlight, where the fox would pause and stare at him from the edge of a field, where the horses would dip their heads like swans.

His cabin. His ranch.

He fingers a thin slice of tree, the one in the pocket of his jeans. He sees in his mind's eye what he knows the paper says.

He's glad his mind's eye will be consistent with what is written on paper, that the two sets flow together. Today, he is tuned in, and he'll stay tuned in as long as he can. When he pulls the slice of tree out, it will be creased and worn to the point he can barely see his penciled marks, but he knows it will list his family.

I am married to Renny.
Carolyn = daughter. Who is married to Del.
Rachel = dead daughter
4 grandchildren: Jack - Leanne (C's) and Billy - Jess (R's)

He fingers the paper because it is calming and stalls the terror. He can sense his own fear of this disease, how it has grown to be a constant companion now, but one on which he still has the upper hand. Today he is winning.

"I built it," he says.

"I know it, Dad. You did a good job. It's a beautiful cabin."

"When Rachel died."

"I know it. It's a nice tight cabin. Dad—"

"It never healed."

She jams her hands into her red coat, takes them out, swings her arms. The fabric makes the swishing sound of water. Then, "What never healed, Dad? Do you mean you? You and Mom?"

"The water is running backwards."

She looks at him, even as they walk, and then says, "If you say so."

"But Jess will take care of it."

She swishes her arms back and forth. "Okay." Her voice is small and quiet like a mourning dove, like the soft gray on a mourning dove's back.

But none of this is what he means. And Carolyn does not mean it's okay, either. He'd like to tell Carolyn the real story.

Not the story that she knows, but the story that registered in his heart. How although he and Renny argued they could also look at the other and know what thoughts were transpiring, what waterways of feeling were moving between them. But then they forgot how to talk. With words or with touch or with eyes. They were silenced. So he moved to the other end of the ranch. He hated and missed his wife. He hated and missed something particular. Perhaps he had no direction, perhaps he had stalled out, perhaps he knew it. Oh, yes. He wants to tell this daughter all this. How can he explain it?

"Dad?" His daughter takes her ball cap off, ponytails her hair, puts the cap back on, and threads her mane of hair through the back. All in one fluid motion, like water.

"Oh," he says. "Oh. Well. That orange twine. That we use to graft calves on to new mothers. I—"

But his daughter is already talking. "Remember that cow we had? I called it Twisted Snout, but everyone else called it Crooked Nose. No, actually, Pablo Picasso. Remember that cow? That cow's nose was bent from the get-go. I'm sorry Mom yelled at you this morning. About the bacon. She's just so . . . tired out, I guess."

"Crooked Nose." He remembers her well. "Yes. She gave birth to Soft Eyes, Crooked Hoof, Wild Mama. Some others." He remembers that Renny yelled at him about the bacon but he can't remember why. Something about needing to put it in a frying pan and not on the burner, but he had put it in a frying pan, hadn't he? Of course he had. Because bacon always needed to go in a pan. He must have just been sleepy. He hates the dark rooms in his brain. He knows they're there, but surely he can also push them into the corner and live in the rest of his brain. "Her sire was X313 and her mama was an Angus-Hereford mix, one of the originals. Pangaea, Renny called her."

9

"Yes!" Carolyn zips and unzips her jacket. "You're exactly right. This ice. You would think it would be white, because of the snow. But no. It's all gray in parts, blue in parts, brown in parts. It's like an ocean. I can't get comfortable. It's too hot and too cold. Too something."

Later she says, "Dad," but she doesn't say more.

They walk in silence, listening to their feet crunch the ice. Walking is slow. Even young Carolyn has to watch her step, only she is not young anymore; she is not a girl, but a woman, but young relatively. When they get to the end of the property, they're at the first rise of the Rocky Mountains, with the startling red-orange cliffs that preface the blue-gray waves of mountains. Here the barbed wire fence stretches across this bulge in the earth, this fence that marks one man's land from another, and they will turn around.

But here is the cabin.

He walks up the steps and onto the porch and peers in the window. It is not locked, there is no reason to lock it, but still he would rather peer in. It looks just as he left it, kitchen table wiped clean except for a pile of slips of papers, a few dishes stacked in the drying rack by the sink. For one year now it has sat empty.

But he feels too tired to ask about that, and so he turns and they start back across the ranch, a two-mile walk. There is a river to their left and a ditch and a county road to their right and the long sprawl of his pastures in between, a long stretch of frozen sea. He loves the aspen trees, both the ones at the edge of the property and the ones he planted near the house. Right now they are bare white trunks with eyes, next to the streak of orange-red willow branches that throb out along the ditch. It is true that willows are the most beautiful thing in the winter. The willows and the backside of the foothills are the only orange-red things out here; the rest is all the white and brown and blues of winter, and he loves that nature thrust in a little bit of strange color. There is a bald eagle roasting or resting or perching or roosting on a branch above the river, which he points to and his daughter says, "Yes, I see it. There are more of them now, aren't there? Some things heal."

His daughter calls the dog whose name sounds like music. The not-retriever dog is rolling in another pile of horse manure and his daughter says, "At least it's frozen." Then, "This is the stupidest winter ever. It's like one great glacier out here, and it's never going to melt." And much later, "Dad? I love you no matter what. No matter what happens. Okay? You've still got some time. It will be hard to know when to . . ." And then later, under her breath, she says, "Ah, god. Fuck." And then, finally, she holds the old wooden gate for him, and although he slows, she stands patiently, insisting that he go first.

RENNY

At the Early Stage Alzheimer Association's Support Group meeting in town, Renny is separated from Ben, which makes her sigh with irritation only because everything makes her sigh with irritation because she is in fact irritated. This is new, this parting of the waters. Ben goes off with the others to make Valentine cards for their caretakers, which is possibly the stupidest thing Renny can think of. Or not stupid, just plain pitiful. Embarrassing. This separation will give caregivers a chance to speak freely, says Esme, the leader, whom Renny really does like. (If only her daughter Carolyn would dress so smartly instead of wearing jeans and T-shirts and a ball cap with a ponytail pulled through the back. And Esme attends church, unlike her daughter. And Esme's name, which is short for Esmeralda, is very pretty; she should have named her daughter Esmeralda.)

Renny sighs and glances around at the other women and men, all white-haired, some fat and some thin, some smart and some seemingly on the verge of the disease themselves. In front of each person at the table is a journal, presented each week so they can vent their frustrations and feelings on paper. She was supposed to decorate hers but instead she just wrote THE SAD STORY OF RENNY AND BEN in thick Sharpie marker on the front. Everyone else cut out pictures of flowers or old automobiles from old-timey newspapers and glued them on the front. She refuses to be reduced to childlike behavior.

Beyond the journals, in the middle of the table, is a plate of cookies. She is so tired of these cheap-brand cookies. No one likes them. Always Lipton tea, which no one likes either. She would like to issue a proclamation to the world: NO ONE IN THE UNIVERSE LIKES LIPTON TEA. Maybe people could stomach the Lipton tea if fresh mint leaves and honey were also provided, but they never are. She wishes she and humanity could both get it right for once. When this winter is over, and summer comes, and the mint springs up next to the farmhouse like weeds—even *then* she will forget the mint every week, and these idiots will still be putting it out, plain, even though no one wants it. She's sure of it, and she will drive Ben to this meeting and forget the mint because her life has always seemed too chaotic and busy to remember basic things like reaching down to grab mint that is right at your feet. She sighs, and then sighs again. She is so tired of the plates with the creased edges, like a pie, only not a pie, only a boring white paper plate. She is tired of this winter.

The truth. The truth. The truth is what Esme wants.

When it is her turn, Renny says one version of it, which is, "If I care for him well, if I stay patient, well, then whatever freak god is out there might let me into heaven. I am only nice because I believe He's watching. I'm afraid of hell. Otherwise I would have flown off to Greece some time ago."

A few others chuckle but she isn't joking. God is a freak—must be, to allow people to suffer like this—and therefore must make freak decisions such as putting people in hell for letting their husbands die of a natural disease. Ben could have died a million times over by now, burning down his house or crashing his truck. Perhaps he would have rotted like a fence post, forgetting to eat. Although, no, he's always hungry, always wanting food, and it's his incessant whining about being hungry that makes her crazy. She wishes she could stay more patient but it's like dealing with a two-year-old, and she didn't even enjoy her daughters at that age—she liked kids when they were older and more self-sufficient and interesting.

At some point people have to die. Ben should just die. But the truth of the matter is that Ben's a good man who still loves his life. She looks around the room, quickly, to mitigate the closing sensation she is having in her throat. She's clarified this emotion with herself many times before: the simultaneous wish for him to die and never die makes her, at times, unable to breathe. The situation is, by its very nature, claustrophobic.

The group is waiting to see if she wants to say more. So she breathes in, acknowledges the panic attack that is threatening her, and smiles sweetly. She will comply to humor them. She says, "This disease is like a yo-yo. Or no, it's much like putting a toe in the river. It's too cold, so you back out, and you try again, you go deeper, you back out, then deeper, and then you are submerged and totally lost. For example, he forgets to fry bacon in a pan and instead puts it right on the stove. But I bet he doesn't do it again. He forgets how to zipper a coat. But then he remembers. Then he's angry for no reason, accusing me of stealing money from his wallet. Then he isn't. One day he couldn't tell time at all. But this week he can. He can't remember that he has four grandchildren, and then he remembers them all, and he even remembers what they are doing. He even remembers to care that they're probably going to turn out rotten. In and out. Pulling in and out of water. Now that I think about it, I think his disease might have set in years ago, the same year our daughter died. Only I didn't notice for a while. But it's moving fast now. We're definitely leaving Stage I. We're moving into Stage II. There's a big difference lately. And he knows it, but he won't know it for much longer. He'll be too underwater to know."

There are murmurs of approval and agreement and sorrow, which makes her feel like a schoolgirl that has gotten an A. She has described it well. "Submerged, yes," someone says, and someone else adds, "Exactly," and someone else apropos of nothing says, "Sometimes this disease reminds me of a Stellar's jay." And Zach, sweet Zach, says, "That was well put, Renny," and winks kindly at her. She tries to stop the smile but it's too late. She curled her hair this morning with pink plastic curlers and she's glad she did that because what- oh-what source of joy is there left for her in this world? She is not interested in men and their sexual needs (oh, what a relief, when she took Ben's hand off her breast decades ago and told him that she was just done with that stuff), but she could use a friend, maybe even a friend that would rub her stiff shoulders and hold her hand, and it might as well be a man since she can't picture wanting a woman to touch her.

Everyone is still smiling at her. Smiling extra hard. She is an honored martyr. She knows that they know. That she has already lost a daughter. And on top of this she has Ben, whose speech and thought has quite suddenly taken a turn for the worse. So she gets an especially high grade for her suffering. And that's what humans want. To feel special. Even for stupid reasons.

Bastards, all of them, she says to herself, to the friendly and smiling faces, all bastards except for maybe Zach. Maybe she hates them all.

She turns to the next person, indicating that it is now *her* turn to tell some freak version of the truth. The woman complies: something about how lonely she is now that she's lost her best friend, which is who her spouse was, and now there's simply no one to talk to over the news anymore . . . Renny sighs and looks out the window where she sees, unsurprisingly, that it is snowing again. This is like Minnesota plopped onto Colorado, and the reason she and Ben chose Colorado, back when such changes were possible and exciting and wonderful, was because Colorado wasn't Minnesota. And yet here they are, in a land of gray misery. This new snow on top of the ice will simply make the ice more dangerous.

She should be more generous but she can't muster the energy. She will not tell the real truth to these people. Or the deepest truth. For there are, of course, many versions, layering on one another like the snow. And the deepest layer is as dangerous as ice underneath. It can kill a person, in fact. The real truth, no. It must be covered with something slightly softer. She has seen the bottle of sodium pentobarbital that Ben no doubt stole from Ruben, when the vet came over to put down the old mother donkey. She's surprised Ben had the presence of mind to do such a thing, only not, because from time to time, his quiet, sharp mind sometimes flickers through. Sometimes his mind is working fine; it's just the words that are dammed up. And it's because of his deep intelligence—she fell in love with him in the first place because he was in fact so bright—that he's able to often find replacement words or different phrases that express what his mind still holds to be true.

Those moments make her so happy.

Ben had hid the bottle very well. But he had also left a note in the pocket of his jeans: PINK JUICE ON TOP SHELF IN BACK ROOM BARN. When she looked, there was in fact a clean bottle and two plastic-wrapped new syringes sitting on a dusty, dark shelf, right alongside coffee cans full of U-nails and dusty orange ear tags. It is breaking her heart. It is cracking her in two. But she must hold steady and strong. She simply will not tell that truth, no.

BEN

He's made Renny a soft pink card with a heart and he forgets why although he remembers that he takes a pill each morning for his heart. On the card he has written THANK YOU because the woman who helped them says that caregivers need that. Renny has thrown the card on the dash of the pickup after sighing and saying "That's nice," and it rests there next to bits of hay and dust and old yellowed receipts from the feed store and curled-up slips of paper and one strand of orange bailing twine. Renny's driving him home now although this is not the right way. They pass a new church that has one of those signs outside, which says COURAGE IS FEAR THAT HAS SAID ITS PRAYERS.

"Stupid big new churches," Renny says.

"Courage is fear . . ." Ben hears himself trailing off, hears his brain trying to make sense of what that means. Now that Renny does all the driving he has more time to look around, which is good. He needs the time. He repeats what the sign said to himself for many minutes before he gets the meaning.

It is a bit like a math problem and he realizes that if you add PRAYER + FEAR, then on the other side of the = sign you get COURAGE. Only it is not exactly addition, it is more complicated than that. Maybe multiplication. He thinks he has it right. But he says, "Amen to that. Go slow. Take it easy. Make sure you know what you're doing, see."

"What?" Renny is squinting, trying to see through the snow. It's a low-temperature snow, small and brittle, coming right at the glass, spitting at them.

"This isn't the way home, Renny."

"We're going to the mall."

"The mall." He does a scan of his brain to remember what a mall is but all he sees is a lot of water. "Is that the remembering room?"

She glances at him. "What? No. I want to walk. It's too icy everywhere and I'm going to fall and break my hip. And then you'll be taking care of me. Or no, Carolyn will, and Carolyn has enough caretaking on her hands. That Jess is going to make her crazy. Jess is worse than any other eighteen-year-old because she isn't *like* an eighteen-year-old. Homeschooled and yet never around. Supposedly bright but never opens her mouth to say something intelligent. She's like a ghost. There is something *wrong* with her, I'm telling you. We're going to walk in the mall. Besides, I need to see some *color.*"

"The mall," he says. "Okay. I could use a bite to eat."

"Ben?"

"I like those sticks of salty—"

"Ben, what's a remembering room?"

But there are no words for it. None that he can remember. Something about how the most simple and basic truth for humankind since ever and ever, which is that we don't want to die. He doesn't want to die, because it scares him. It scares him because he doesn't know what comes next. And also because he's wary that some horrible god will judge him this way or that. Or for killing. He hates that god anyway, that's a fact, although now he can't remember why, although oh yes he does, he remembers now, he remembers it's because that god let his daughter die. God let Jess's mother die.

Except that there's one moment in space where sometimes there is a remembering room. It offers a moment of peace. If only he can find it. The only god he loves is the god of the remembering room. It's the god who made the ranch, the god who made nature, the god who made willows and bald eagles, and that god is different than the one who likes to watch people suffer.

He looks to Renny to say something, but Renny says, "You could *always* use a bite to eat. You're going to drive me crazy. Why don't you quit thinking about yourself for once? Think of something nice you could do for someone else. Go to one of Jess's barrel races."

"But Jess . . . doesn't barrel race anymore . . ."

"Well, that's true." But Renny is distracted, squinting into the snow, trying to make a turn. "Go sit with her, then, like you used to. Take her fishing." Then he hears Renny sigh, and it is an important kind of sigh. It means, *I'm sorry I said that, I know you can't tie a hook on a line or release the line at the right time, and I'm sorry I said that, I'm always saying things like that.* He knows what she means and so he reaches over to touch her knee. Renny glances at him, offers a small smile. "Jess is going to end up pregnant and on welfare. Nobody that quiet is going to end up *normal*, that's for sure. I wonder what goes on in her head all day. Don't you think it's weird, that she's always hanging around, but not really there? It's spooky."

He reminds himself to be quiet, and he says, "I know, I should just be quiet," and she says, "Ben, that's not what I'm saying," and he says, "We're both quiet."

He stares into the streaked mirror that has been put on the sun visor in front of him. He sees a man who is not really him. This man is too old. This man has white short hair, a dirty Angus Breeders' Association ball cap, blue eyes. This man has a scar on his cheekbone from the time a mastitis-filled heifer charged him. This man has gray stubble that hasn't been shaved. And yet, there he is, the same self who has been with him all along. The boy who ran along creek beds, so alive. His eyes water from the simple fact that this is him, but not him. The space between those two facts hurts his heart. Like a math problem that can't be worked out, that has no solution.

He stares ahead into the snow and directs his mind—he can still do that—to recall the animals he's helped put down in his life. It's wrong to see things suffer. He has buried dogs. He has shot dying horses in the head, and he did a good job, except the one that flailed about so long it made his heart shudder. He has put animals out of misery, which was the right thing to do. He has also killed to eat—he's hunted elk and geese and taught his daughters to do so. He has gutted fish. He has helped the rendering man load up dead and bloated cows, some of them pregnant. He has shot prairie dogs and fox for no good reason back when he was younger although he stopped doing that years ago because he figured they had a right to live on his land too. He even once shot Renny's peacock down from a tree because it would not stop honking and although he thinks of himself as a calm man he has sometimes lost his temper. They had just fought and her peacock was as noisy and horrible as she was. He has killed. He has killed many things. Mostly out of mercy, but some not.

Through the snow, he sees the Greyhound bus station. A bus has just pulled up. A dog on the front of the bus is running, running, and he wishes the dog could curl up and sleep. Especially in a blizzard. "We could go somewhere warm," he says.

"We're going to the mall, which is warm." Renny sighs a frustrated sigh.

"I mean, we could go for a long time."

"A trip? A vacation?"

"Yes! To that place with tall rocks like silos."

Renny puts her hand to her head and moans.

He knows he should be quiet. He means Utah, but now it's too late to say it.

It's because of the horse he shot once—the horse that needed to be put down and he used a hollow-tipped bullet that didn't quite do the job and the horse stumbled around and crashed into fences. Because of that horse, he stole the pink juice from the vet. An animal deserves to die a clean, painless death, and he won't ever use a gun again, or at least not now, when his aim might be bad. He will use a gun as backup—it's always important to have a backup—but he will always be as gentle as possible. He wrote down the dose on a note in his pocket although he has known this dose for a very long time. He won't forget it, but still.

"The vet?" he says now.

"Ruben."

"Yes, Ruben. I just feel . . . sorry. He—"

"Oh, Ben. He'll be fine."

"But I—"

"Ben!" She says it sharply and gives him a look, one that means he is to be quiet now. He presses his lips together and at the same time sees Renny opens her mouth to speak—some objection—but then closes it. Like a fish that is dying. Like one he will soon gut. Only he doesn't want to gut Renny, because, in fact, Renny has already been gutted by life. By a dead daughter. And he will not—he will *not*—gut her again by being the kind of burden that he is becoming.

The mall, he finds, is a big bright building. It has a fountain in the middle into which children throw pennies. He hates this place because it is not outside with willows and stretches of grass-ocean.

Renny charges ahead and he trots to follow.

"Tell you what I'm gonna do, see. I remember Rachel."

"What are you talking about?" Renny yells it and then stops and looks down at herself, brushes her pants off as if removing something, as if she is reentering the world. "Please for god's sake try to make sense, Ben," she says, more quietly.

It stuns him sometimes, how cruel she can be. "I remember." He says it in a whisper.

"Just please be quiet." Renny charges on ahead. "I need some peace and quiet." But then she turns around on her heels and says, "I want to stop at that place. You like their carrot salad more than you like their fries."

He does not remember ever having a carrot salad. He does like the salty sticks which are called fries. Renny orders for him and he feels like a child behind her, wanting to say that he would prefer that kind of drink that's made from a root and is sweet and tangy but instead she is ordering him lemonade. That's okay, because lemonade is fine too.

He fingers the paper in his pocket. He tells people, "The body is fine but the brain's not working so good." He feels proud of this clever statement to explain it all, now that his brain is not a private matter anymore. He can't remember what the church sign said, but it was good. It was important. He sometimes can't read the shorthand comments he writes on paper although he remembers that they made sense when he wrote them down. The paper in the pocket of his jeans makes sense, though. It says:

Dose: 1 cc per 10 lbs.
Dose: 20 ccs. (But use more)

Pink juice is cleaner and faster and more sure. Although his vet did tell him the story of how he once put down a New-foundland dog with it; the family buried it in a pasture, and by morning the dog had dug its way out, which is why the vet stays extra long to make sure that the heart has stopped. Exactly. The vet had stayed extra long with the donkey, making sure she was really dead, which is how Ben grabbed the bottle from his vet bag and put it in the deep pocket of his Carhartt jacket. He's sorry he did that to the vet.

He has to be fair with himself. That's what the nice woman at the meetings says. Think of the *good* that you did, she says. Think of the things that made you *valuable*. Think of the things you put *in motion*.

And so he remembers: He has birthed many things too. Foals and calves and kittens and puppies. He has reached inside heifers and turned calves. He has saved slick newborns by blowing his own breath into their lungs. He has wiped away suffocating mucus. He has given vaccinations and antibiotics that healed. He has let trout go, after removing the hooks. He untangled an antelope from a barbed wire fence once and watched it lope off, unharmed. He has snapped muskrat and beaver traps, when he came upon them along the streambeds of his youth. He has doctored horses through colic and he has punctured the bloat out of cows.

He has saved far more lives than he has taken, and saving takes longer than killing. A great amount of time in a rancher's life is about reducing suffering—that he has always been clear on—and he was a good rancher.

He can do it. "I can do it," he says to Renny, and tries to catch her eye.

He wonders if she knows, somehow, what he's saying, because she reaches across the table and puts her hand over his, and both hands tremble on their own. Perhaps old age, he thinks, or a small refusal to flinch from fear.

RENNY

As soon as her daughter Carolyn opens her truck's door, the dog jumps out and runs around the yard at top speed in loopy circles, woofing and leaping on imaginary mice hidden in the new deep snow. It runs through the aspen trees and then squats and pees, leaving a yellow blotch on the pure white. It takes off after the chickens, sending them squawking and running, and it runs over to the donkey and barks, which causes the donkey to raise his head and let out an ear-shattering hee-haw of disgust. All this before Carolyn can unfold herself from the truck and walk to the front door. Renny sees all this from the kitchen window, and when Carolyn walks in, stomping her feet, Renny says, "Your dog needs sedation."

"She's still a puppy, Mom. Cut her some slack." Carolyn sets down a bag of groceries and examines a new long red welt on her hand, probably from the dog scrambling past her. "Yelapa, Mexico. Bought the tickets today. Tiny little village accessible only by burro and water taxi. No cars. Figured that our first real vacation ought to be a unique one. Do you remember what it feels like to be overjoyed with life?"

"No."

"Me neither. But that dog does." But Carolyn is smiling to herself as she begins unpacking the brown paper bag. Then she is digging in the cupboard's disorganized mess for the right pans, and in a split second she is stirring the honey and oil on the stove top. Carolyn has always done everything fast. The way she empties the dishwasher or throws potatoes into a roast or digs a fence post. Fast, but not thoughtless. Fast only because that's how you raise four kids and run a ranch and manage life. You go fast, or you get buried.

"I should have named you Esmeralda," says Renny. "Go use your own stove."

"That's a good name," Carolyn says. "My stove is broken."

"You would have turned out better."

"Probably."

"Names mean a lot."

"They do."

"Quit being so agreeable. You're just like your father."

"All right."

"And Jess."

"Jess is fine. Considering."

"Jess is going to end up pregnant and on welfare."

"Oh, Mom. Cut it out. Haven't we already made a wager on this matter?" Carolyn turns and raises an eyebrow at her, but there is a playful look in her eye. "The new stove gets delivered next week. Don't worry."

Renny snorts. "I don't know why you're in a good mood. What's wrong with you?" Then, "Maybe we should trade caretaking. You can have Ben, and I'll take Jess. I'll make her talk and communicate like a normal person. And you can be your sweet patient self with Ben."

Carolyn is cutting open a bag of slivered almonds. "Mom, I already told you that you can move Dad into my house. I'll try it. He can have Billy's old room."

Renny starts sorting her spice rack. The little red and white boxes are so old and grimy with kitchen grease and dust that she should just throw them out. Some of them are ten years old. She does not like cooking. She does not like spices. She does not like people and their incessant needs. "You say that, but he will ruin your life. You'll end up getting divorced. And you don't have enough time for him, Carolyn. You'd have to take him everywhere, and you wouldn't get anything done. Your ranch will fall apart, your marriage will fall apart, your sanity will fall apart."

Now Carolyn is cutting open a bag of wheat germ, and it makes Renny crazy, how healthy Carolyn has become. All of a sudden this interest in fish oil and vitamin B and wheat germ. Trying to stave off dementia, she knows. Renny picks five spices that she knows she hasn't used in at least a year and throws them in the trash.

"Turmeric," Carolyn says, as she glances from the trash can to Renny. "Turmeric helps stave off dementia. Don't throw it away."

Then Carolyn opens her mouth to say something else, stops, starts, stops. Renny thinks she looks like a fish gasping for air, and it makes Renny's heart do an odd flutter. She loves Carolyn, actually, which is why she wouldn't let her take Ben in. She wants Carolyn to have some semblance of a life.

Renny hears Ben singing from the bedroom *cool, clear, water.* He must be up from his nap. She turns and watches Ben come out of the bedroom, stop at the dining room table, stare down at his white scrawny legs. She can see him pause, see him register the fact that he is without his jeans. Sees his indecision. Sees him working through the situation. Sees him, thank god, turn around. She hates him. She pities him. She's sorry. She's angry. She's grateful he knew enough to return to the bedroom.

Carolyn is stirring the oats and wheat germ, yakking away mindlessly in her stupid good-natured way. Just like the dumb dog, who now wants to come in, but instead of decisively barking, as a normal dog would, it offers a mediocre whine outside the door. Renny sighs and lets the dog in and, meanwhile, watches Carolyn move about the kitchen.

"Mom, this is the first winter in twenty years that we can leave the ranch. The kids are all fine. Billy is in Europe for another two weeks, and Jess will go stay with Leanne. Del and I want one vacation. Can you watch Satchmo?"

Renny watches the dog track muddy snow globs across her kitchen floor and sighs her new favorite kind of sigh, which is when she vibrates her lips together so that she sounds a little like an irritated horse. Carolyn, her daughter. In a baggy stained white T-shirt with CHEYENNE FRONTIER DAYS cheaply ironed on the front and jeans and dirtied tennis shoes. Carolyn, her daughter. With no makeup and a red nose from a cold and the same ponytail hairdo she's had since she was a teenager, only now streaked with gray. Carolyn, her daughter, who probably hasn't giggled in, well, Renny doesn't know how long. She knows her daughter deserves a vacation and yet why does her daughter get to go on vacation? Both are simply true at once. *She'd* like to go to some little village in Mexico.

Carolyn is now standing over the stove, pouring a capful of vanilla into a pan, and then scraping the last of the honey from the mason jar, moving the reluctant crystallized globs. "Mom?

Del and I need this. Need it. I realize you need a vacation too. Take one when we're back. I'll come and stay over here with Dad. He should stay. Travel will confuse him. But where do *you* want to go? A cruise? A flight? What would *you* like to do on your own? Besides this ranch? What makes you happy?"

Renny turns away from the honey—something about it is so beautiful that her heart hurts—and looks down at the dog on her kitchen floor. The last time she was single and free was nearly fifty years ago, back when she'd enrolled at the university, was studying agricultural sciences, even a little Spanish, helped out at the 4-H club, and met Ben, and she can't remember that younger hopeful version of herself, can't remember what it felt like, can't remember when she noticed that all those doors had closed, can't fathom how it will be to be single again. The truth is, she has no idea what she wants to do now. It's not that she hasn't thought about it. It's just that nothing seems right.

The dog is on its back, its belly exposed, its front teeth bared, wanting a belly rub. "Your dog is a mutant," she says, and then she takes the pork chops from the refrigerator and starts to trim the fat off. "The only good thing about my life is the fact that I have a Cutco knife."

Carolyn glances at the knife and then at the pork chop. "Okay. Where's Dad?"

"He's getting dressed. Take him on a walk. I think your oven probably works fine. You're just coming up with excuses to come over here so you don't have to live your own life. You think you're checking up on us. But really, you're just bothering us, Carolyn. I don't want to watch your dog. I'm *busy*. My hands are *full*."

"Mom, come *on*. Anton is coming over to feed the cattle and everything, and he's got Ruben as backup. Satchmo can't stay alone in the house all day. That's cruel. I've got everything else taken care of. And believe me, Mom, my oven is *broken*. I want to make granola and my oven is broken. I don't know why you won't *leave*, Mom. Go with a tour group. Go with me. Go alone. You're acting like a martyr."

Renny snorts. "I wish. That would be a luxury."

"A martyr who is roasting at the stake. But every once in a while you take hunks of burning logs and fling them at people."

"What's *that* supposed to mean?"

"It means you're a mean and bitter martyr."

"For heaven's sake. I am not." And then, because Carolyn's comment has made her cranky, she adds, "At least I'm not mean with silence, like Jess."

"Jess's silence is not mean, Mom."

"All silence is mean."

Carolyn tilts her head. "Mainly, I agree with you. But her silence is simply watchfulness. She's eighteen. She's like Satchmo. She's young. She's been through a lot. Cut them both some slack."

"No," Renny says, throwing out a few more spice cans. "I will not." She turns from the pork chops and watches Carolyn stir the melting honey-oil-vanilla in with the oats, and she can see that Carolyn is also delighted at the simple beauty of liquid honey. That's one nice thing about Carolyn that Renny has always liked: her simple curiosity and appreciation for small wonders. Rachel never had that, even as a child. Rachel demanded too much. She expected things to be beautiful, or perhaps just didn't even notice if they were or were not. But Carolyn noticed, noticed from the very get-go.

"Look at that," Carolyn raises her spoon, watching the honey fall in a cascade down into the pan, and smiles a calm smile. "Mom? I had a nightmare the other night. I couldn't get any words out, my throat wouldn't work, and I was so scared.

I just needed to say something and I couldn't and so I was trapped, really trapped. I woke up and thought, 'God, is this what he feels like?' Does he tell you what it's like?"

Renny looks in the cupboard and pulls out a can of green beans. Back when she loved her family, and there was a family to love, and back when Ben was there to smile over a dinner gone right, she grew beans and froze them herself. She hasn't had a garden in a decade; all that work for naught. None of those fresh vegetables helped his brain. Or his heart. "Sometimes he talks about it. Once he said it was like being on a horse. First, like the disease was like being on a horse that was walking. And then trotting. And it is turning into a gallop. An out-and-out run." She leans to look out the window. "And I am not a mean martyr. I have a fundamental spark. Jess does not. In that way, she reminds me of Rachel, and I worry she's going to end up like Rachel."

"Well, Mom, it's nice you care. Just be gentler."

"Gentle gets nothing done." Renny looks out the window and sees the horses gallop up to stand in the vee of the fence. Their breath mists out, one of them shakes, and one nuzzles the other's hindquarters. They are involved in some sort of game, known only to them, and it makes them happy, and that makes them beautiful.

Carolyn looks over her shoulder and sees them too. "So, Mom? Dad sees clearly that it's coming? The disease is galloping into his mind?"

"I think more that his mind is galloping into the disease."

Carolyn pours a canister of oats into a roasting pan and then a bag of almonds, then pours the melted honey over the oats and almonds. "And so he knows."

"What? That he's dying? Dying a first death, before a second? Yes, he knows. He knows it's going to be horrible. And it is,

Carolyn. It is." And suddenly, deeply, so much that it makes her gasp, Renny wants to tell Carolyn about the sodium pentobarbital. She opens her mouth, closes it. Feels her throat tighten. No, she won't. She won't do it. Because it's Ben's choice, and because it *is* that much of a hell, and Ben is trapped and scared and she can feel it. And because some silence is a gift. Instead, she finds herself saying, "I'll watch your damn dog. While you go to Mexico."

The corner of Carolyn's mouth lifts, but still she is silent. A few of the oats fall out and sizzle at the bottom of the oven.

"It bothers me too, Mom. That Ray has been let out of prison. 'Earned time.' We all wish for a bit of that." Then she whispers, "That's why I need to go, right now, and get out of here. If Ray is free, I need to go. I swear, in certain ways, that guy keeps killing us all."

BEN

Is it possible they know? He stands in the living room, trying to size up the situation. Renny is speaking to Carolyn in a calm, cadenced voice, and the surprise of this startles him into stopping. He has always thought of himself as an alert deer, ears lifted for the details, to avoid Renny's usual oncoming crashness. He smiles, and then smiles because he has not, after all, forgotten to smile, and because he has not forgotten how to observe and mark the measure of a man or a moment.

He has had his entire life to prepare for death, and he remembers, as a boy, a preacher telling the congregation exactly that. He sat between his parents in the small church in Greeley and stared at the filtered light and his mother took his hand. When you arrive at the door of death, the preacher had said, your main job is to open the door with courage and the sure knowledge that you have lived well and that you have become yourself. Let death find you with your chin up, your eyes steady.

His mind holds that moment perfectly; not one detail is missing. On this topic, he can think clearly. It pains him that he has fallen short of that goal. Fear bloomed as he got older, bloomed more at his diagnosis. From time to time, too, he has failed in courage. When his daughter died, when he built his cabin. Those were times he flinched. Perhaps the preacher could have advised him on what to do in that case. Perhaps the younger version of him should have been less confident that he'd meet death with his chin up.

He and Renny have never healed. They *had* loved each other, when the ranch was new and they worked, side by side, buying cattle, putting up fences, doctoring calves. Then came their newborn daughters, who grew into toddlers that waddled after chickens and threw rocks at fresh piles of manure. Then their daughters grew up, arguing themselves through their teenage years, and yet so interesting that he felt as if he could stare at them forever. Then one died. He built a cabin. He and Renny lived on opposite ends of the ranch. This is when he felt both the lovely grace of solitude and the frightening qualities of empty sound. It feels now like a sin. He should have said he was sorry. He'd been too stubborn and cowardly to ever properly apologize, and this has been the greatest sin of all.

Five years ago, Renny tells him. He stares into the kitchen and stares at the spot on the floor where they all got axed apart. Like a round of wood being split. Rachel's pickup in the driveway, her running to him, her mouth open trying to speak. Ben was frozen. He had been reading to Renny while she cooked. He stood. His mouth opened. Rachel's eyes, so scared, so full of suffering. He looked past Rachel to Ray. He'll never understand that. How he stood, and froze, and looked. And even after the gun shattered the air and his daughter still, he was frozen.

His daughter that died left behind two kids, and he remembers their names today, Jess and Billy, which gives him the rotting sense of hope that his mind will clear and words will come and appear on his tongue as they should, and that the tip of his tongue will grow back as it should. The daughter he hears talking in the kitchen raised her own two kids, plus Rachel's two kids, like a mother cow that has a grafted calf or two. A good mother.

He thinks to go into the kitchen, with the two talking women, but he stays put, hiding. They're talking about him. He stops, stares at his slippers. He's wearing a colorful Western shirt, with button snaps, because they are easier. Gray pants. Yes, he is all dressed.

But something is missing, something important. He backs up, quietly, turns back around, toward the bedroom. Something is at the edges of his mind, but he can't quite catch it. Then he remembers: There is one bad thing he's done he can't undo, and one he can.

He has to write it down before he forgets. He finds a notebook on his dresser and a pencil and writes it:

1. Genes. Watershed. Can't fix.
2. Ray. Water runs backward. Fix.

He sits on his bed and stares at the dark wall of his bedroom. Ranchers know genes; he bred his cattle to exhibit certain traits. In fact, he knew more about EPDs than most anyone. Expected Progeny Differences. How to determine the traits of the sire's offspring. He knows that he has bad DNA. Bad genes. He has been the watershed. He has been the source. And god how he hopes that the water has been pure. He never meant.

The other danger. Ray.

He needs the slip of paper that tells him *where and how to get there*. He stands up and digs around until he finds it, in yesterday's jeans, and slips it into the pocket of the pants he's wearing. He must be careful.

Funny how he wasn't angry with Ray while Ray was in Cañon City prison. Not angry, just sad. His brain never considered Ray much. When he was in prison, Ray used to write notes of apology and memories and excuses and send them to Ben and Renny. Renny used to tack them up at Violet's Grocery alongside the HAY FOR SALE and FREE KITTENS signs and it was some need of hers to communicate this thing that was tearing her apart. But he found it inappropriate, as he did most of Renny's behaviors, and he would drive to the grocery and take them down. That he remembers.

But then last week they heard that Ray had been released. Del told them. Second-degree murder charges, is that what they were called? A class 2 Felony. Time was up. Or not really. How many years for one life? But there was earned time. Good behavior. No one, not even the judge, can accurately calculate the sentence. Like a math problem that can't be solved. Like a life. No one can calculate. No one knows. Del had sat them down at the kitchen table and said all this. He had presented them with a waxed bag with two Fern's Very Famous Cinnamon Rolls and had said, "Renny and Ben, I wanted to tell you. Jess and Billy know. You've probably been notified, or you will be. But I wanted to tell you myself. Ray's been released from prison. His time was up. He's going to Greeley—" and here Del glances at Ben, because Ben was born and raised in Greeley, and then he adds, "Just thought you should know."

A switch flipped, then. Ben couldn't help it, but he started having conversations with Ray in his head each day, all day. He says, *Out, Ray, out,* but Ray is still in his brain. Ever since

Del told them, he has been walking and saying *Out Out Out* and walking more and saying *Out Out Out* and yet Ray has moved into his brain. Ray has moved into his brain, right next to the disease.

The conversations fill his mind like chickadees coming in for bread crumbs, always there, always there even when you try to shoo them away.

Out, coward.

Out, bully.

Out, small man. Drinking too much. Depressed. Feckless. So you say. But why? Because you're selfish.

Too lazy to be a good human. Lazy coward.

He heard something in that meeting he goes to that is not true. The woman said that it's very hard for people losing their memory to realize when they're moving into the new stage, the one where you don't remember that you have a remembering problem. But that is not true. He can tell. It is happening now, and he can tell how little time he has left. He knows. He knows he has to hurry. So that he can have this conversation for real. He wants to hold Ray up to his face and say it all. He will tell Ray all these conversations and then they will be out of his brain.

He will finally say these words. He will get them out of his brain. Because courage is fear that has said its prayers. The perfect words come to him in a flash.

He has already prayed and asked forgiveness from the universe. If he has upset the natural order of things. He has nearly forgiven himself. He has always been a gentle man, and in part, that has been the problem. He must rise up and be fierce for once. He has asked forgiveness for his gentleness and not fighting more for Rachel to come home, for not fighting when Rachel raced into his house, for not noticing fast enough that

Ray had a gun and was raising it, and for tackling Ray three seconds too late (exactly three because he has counted so many times), and that he has not done more good in his life. At least he can do this.

He has this disease with his brain—he can't remember what it's called—and he knows it gets worse. That's why Renny moved him back to the farmhouse, made him leave his little cabin. He remembers that room, how Renny found scraps of paper in his kitchen and stared at them a long time and said *oh god, oh god*. The names of his friends and the vet and his address and his hometown. He heard *oh god oh god* and he had been ashamed and scared. That is when she took him to the doctor who studies brains and she dumped the slips on the doctor's desk. The doctor asked him so many questions that his head hurt and then the doctor said, "I'm sorry," and then talked about a drug called Aricept (for some reason he can remember that) but he had not taken it because Renny, at her computer, had read things that made her worry.

"A stupid crapshoot," she had said.

"A stupid crapshoot," he says now. Meaning not just the brain drug, but life. Although he reminds himself over and over that he got dealt a fairly good hand. Not great, but good. He could do without this disease, and he could do without a dead daughter, but the rest has been a fairly good hand.

"We sure helped a lot of things be born." He says this when he walks into the kitchen, to his wife and daughter. They both turn and smile at him. Beautiful smiles in a warm kitchen. By god if he's going to gut his wife and daughter like a fish.

But he needs to hurry. He can feel the slip now, fast as a dam breaking and the sudden onslaught of water.

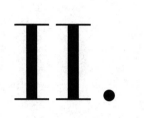

II.

"My tongue will tell the anger of my heart, or else my heart concealing it will break."

—WILLIAM SHAKESPEARE

The Taming of the Shrew (act 4, scene 3)

RENNY

She feeds the chickens, who are as annoyed with the winter as she. They have quit laying eggs nearly altogether, as if in protest, and eye her as if she's responsible for the short days and bad weather. She scowls back. None of this winter is her idea. She's done what she can to mitigate and help. She's even put in a light that flicks on at four in the morning, and she's given them extra vitamins, and their egg production should not, in fact, be so low. She does try, she does. Just as she feeds Ben. She does lather his face in the mornings, she does do his laundry, she does show him how to turn on the radio, she does drive him somewhere at least twice a week to get him out of the house. A thousand acts of kindness each day, for Ben and the chickens and the donkeys and the horses and she *does* do so much.

And no one loves her, not even the chickens, and no one notices, and no one cares.

"Give me an egg or two, girls." She murmurs this to them in the cold-echo air of the cement-block chicken house, and in response, a mouse runs along the baseboard of the floor. She slides her hand under each chicken, each sitting in her own nesting box, and they gently peck her hand in protest. Fat Girl has one under her; Penny does not.

She stares at the globe in her hand. E-G-G. It should stand for something. Or maybe not. All the stupid acronyms in the world. People and their stupid need for letters. The Department of Corrections, DOC. Average length of stay, ALOS. Provisions of section 18-1.3-406. Colorado Murder in the Second Degree. The SORL1 protein. The NIA, National Institute on Aging. The NHGRI, the National Human Genome Research Institute. She wonders if Carolyn and the kids should get tested. They could let their hopes sink to the depth of the sea, where they belong. They can have their hearts be broken now, and get it over with. There is, in fact, some sense in that.

Perhaps someone in this family has it. Jess, probably. All that she has in common with him. Please let them not share that. Please, no.

One of the chickens near the end of the row lets out a cackle of egg-laying, and so she stands there, in the cold, waiting. Life is about efficiency. This chicken is the one that Jess once named Oh-Beetle-Beetle, and she hardly pecks at all. Not like Floppy, who can bring tears.

The beta-amyloid proteins. The presenilin 1, or PS1, genes and how they affect lysosomes, how they get mutated. She's never been stupid. She's kept books and invested well and guessed correctly when to cut the hay. She had a degree in animal sciences, but she was born in the wrong era—she just got married, without thinking about it—and she should have gone on to be a vet or a scientist. But she was good at the business side of the ranch, and she kept the books, and she made up her own useful acronyms or codes. She wonders if she could ever tell a friend—perhaps Zach?—about all this. How her love for the ranch was manifested by making it *work*. By knowing all the words and columns and figures and facts.

She stamps her feet to warm up, glides her hand over the chicken, and then notices, with a start, how clean the chicken house is. The cement floor is mostly devoid of chicken shit; there's only the clean hay that has been kicked around by the chickens themselves. It's clean enough, in fact, that she knows it must have been cleaned today. She pauses, cocks her head. "Jess?" She calls it out, in the cool air of the chicken house, and then leans her head out the door and calls it again.

She stares into the silence created by the boom of her voice. A squirrel has paused halfway up a tree. The donkeys have raised their heads. The hayfields and distant mountains all sit in silent white. And then she hears the clink of hoof on wood, and she walks out of the chicken house and into the shed next door, the one in which they stack the best hay and alfalfa, and she sees Jess in there with Fury, the horse, both in the space created by missing bales, in a cavern created by still-green hay. The horse is standing, shifting his weight, but Jess is sitting on a bale, leaning against another bale, just *lying* there, in a ratty old sleeping bag, looking as if she's dozing. She's wearing a gray flannel shirt that used to belong to Ben and a Carhartt jacket and a bright pink hand-knitted hat that someone in the Alzheimer's support group made for her. She looks up at Renny with one eye.

"Warming up," she says. "Smells good in here."

"*Why* do you have a sleeping bag in a hay shed?"

Jess rubs her nose and shrugs.

"There's a *house* for warming up. You could come *inside*."

"I like it here."

Renny simply doesn't know what to do with blankness. "You just carry a sleeping bag around with you?" She cocks her head and stares. It's true that Jess is beautiful, more beautiful than anyone in the family. Fine dark brown hair and green eyes with eyelashes long enough to belong on a horse. A perfect dimple on one side, which rarely shows. Tall and slender and beautiful. A lot like Rachel, except that Jess has a still-noble presence and a quiet watchfulness that is like Ben. And it's this centeredness—Renny decides that's the right word—that gives Jess her deep beauty, which is shining so bright right now that Renny has to scowl at it, otherwise she will gasp.

"Well, yes. On the saddle."

Jess always speaks with the tone of voice that ends conversations, no upward lilt, no invitation to keep speaking. She's done speaking, and Renny would like to strangle her. Instead, she pauses, breathes, tries to make her voice more pleasant. "Was it you that cleaned the chicken house?" And when Jess nods affirmative with a shrug, Renny nods at the room, then at Jess, which is her way of saying thanks. "Well, why aren't *you* going to Mexico? They could take you."

Jess gives her a look of amused delight. "Goodness, Renny. It's a romantic getaway. Plus, I don't want to go."

"Why not?"

"Because I want to be here right now."

"And why is that?"

Jess shrugs, as if it's obvious. Then she says, "Renny, you're all right."

Renny lets the horse nuzzle her jacket, which makes a swishing noise. "You want to be here, in this cold wasteland of an idiot winter, and stay by yourself in that house, and not go to Mexico, and not come stay with us. Do I have that right, Jess?"

"Yes," Jess says.

Renny hears the gruff of her voice, and she tries to calm it. "Jess, I don't understand you. Not one bit."

"I like it here."

"But no *normal person* would like it here, Jess."

Jess shrugs.

"Why don't you go talk to Grandpa, at least?"

"I just did. He went past me on his way on a walk, so I walked with him to the middle gate. He was talking about gutting fish. How we used to fish together and he'd gut the fish for me, because I didn't like it. He didn't like gutting fish either, it turns out. I didn't know that."

Renny reaches out to stroke Fury's neck. The horse, at least, is deserving of some attention. But she will try. "I remember how surprised I was, when you first moved here, after Rachel, that you'd never been fishing." When Jess only nods, Renny adds, "You were just a young teenager, of course, but I suppose I had thought Ray or Rachel had taken you. You lived right by that lake!"

Jess chews on a piece of hay, looks up. "Nope, we never went fishing."

"Ben loved doing that with you. After you moved here."

"I know."

"Ben was a good grandfather."

"I know."

"What was Ray or Rachel thinking, never taking two kids fishing?"

"I wish Ray wasn't getting out." Jess says it while looking up at dust motes floating in the sunlight coming through the door. "Does stress make Alzheimer's worse? Ever since last week, Grandpa has seemed . . . worse. I wonder if Ray stresses him out."

She says it calmly and quietly, rhetorically, and it suddenly occurs to Renny that she simply hasn't thought about how all this must feel to Jess. Not really. How it would feel to be in Jess's body. How people keep disappearing on her. How it would feel to have your mother's killer, your stepfather, free from jail? And your mother gone? And your grandfather disappearing? And would you worry that this killer-father would try to get in touch with you? Does she ever get angry at how unfair it all is? At the same time, she wonders at herself for not wondering sooner. Why don't thoughts like this occur to her naturally? Why has she not considered this before? It's like forgetting mint for Lipton tea. She wonders if some segment has always been missing from her brain. What's wrong with *her*? She will get better at this; she will try for a real conversation.

"All this time," Renny says, "I've been able to picture Ray in a cell, eating food from a metal rectangular plate. And now? Now he is in Greeley, Colorado, doing what? Ordering pie? Applying for jobs? Now that he's out, well, what will he do? Men like that need to exert control. They need familiar surroundings. They'll apologize and then become assholes again. Jess, he was so . . . feckless. So unmindful. I guess I hadn't thought how that would feel . . ."

Jess shrugs, but her peaceful look is gone. She unzips the sleeping bag, stands up, brushes hay off her jeans. "I'm gonna ride home—"

"I doubt he'll directly contact us. He hasn't been in touch with you, has he?" She pauses. "You're not worried, are you?"

"No." Jess glides her hand along the horse's neck, twines her fingers in the mane. Renny notices Jess's efficiency, just like Carolyn, but one heartbeat calmer and smoother. She watches as Jess folds up the sleeping bag, sets it on a bale of hay, and slides the reigns into her hands. She pulls the horse forward, nudging gently past Renny so she can get out the door, like a ghost that's going to walk through her. Renny steps to the side and watches them both clomp past her.

"Well, good-bye," she calls after Jess, who has mounted and started to ride in the direction of her own house.

Jess puts up a hand in a silent wave, and Renny resists the urge to pick up a hunk of icy snow and throw it at her head. And then she does, but the clump falls short, and neither the horse nor the rider acknowledges the soft sound behind them of snow falling into snow.

She walks back into the chicken house, reaches under the chicken, past the fluff, past the pecks on her hand, and brings out another the egg. Now she has two.

As she walks back to the ranch house, it starts to snow. She realizes that Ben might have been the one who knew the water best—his endless days out there with a shovel and plastic dams, his endless musing over the best ways to cover a field with irrigation water. But it was she who understood the facts and figures. Which is why she knows about Apolipoprotein E-e4, which is called simply APOE-e4, but she likes knowing the long version. She likes knowing about the gene variants of CR1, CLU, and PICALM, and a fifth gene variant, BIN1, which is so genetically important. Alzheimer's.

It comes to her then: She knows this ranch like a chart. But Ben knows it like a poem. She hopes he's the wiser one, because it gives her permission to leave it up to him to make the right decision.

BEN

Ben stands in his darkened bedroom and cannot remember why he's there. He is next to his bed, looking down at his suitcase. It's like a cave, this room, dark, with stalagmites of cracks in the plaster, with the old thick original window that is buckled and warped because the glass has turned to water.

On the shelf, there is a photo of his mother and father and sister, all dead. He used to work cattle with them at the old place in Greeley, and he remembers well how they'd run cows in the corral before sending them through the chute. He remembers the onion crop and the sugar beets. He remembers that it is a town founded on the idea of irrigation, that a man, long ago—Horace Greeley, his name was—had thought to build a utopian community on the plains. How another man—James Michener, his name was—wrote a book called *Centennial*. And if he remembers correctly, that author got it about right. About the hardships and the dust and the hopes and the calloused hands of working the desert into fruition.

But in certain ways, he wonders if moving all that water was ruining the earth even as they watered it into being. The balance got upset.

There's a funny thing, he's realizing. Which is that his mind is just like the cows in the vee of a fence. He has cornered his diseased mind and he can separate from it and give it vaccinations. He can observe it and keep records of it, as he would a cow. But someday it will come out of the corner and meet up with the rest of his mind and he won't be able to corner it any longer. Like a heifer gone berserk; no keeping her in.

He told Renny he was taking a nap. But the truth is, the time has come.

Greeley, Colorado. He writes it down on a notepad, because now he remembers why he's standing by his bed. He knows that things with many steps get hard. Lists are good. For example, the story of the woman in his disease group who used to make biscuits—she loved biscuits!—but then there were too many steps. Now she has to use Bisquick even though she does not like Bisquick. She holds his hands at the meetings and he always wonders if she feels angry at the boxed biscuits.

He has made a good list, and that's important because there are lots of things to think through. The list is in his suitcase. He consults it now and doesn't move on to the next item until he is sure. He has packed clothing, his Colt .45, bullets, the pink juice, syringes, money (which he has stolen from Renny, because she thinks he doesn't know fives from fifties and doesn't let him carry cash anymore). He has written a note with his name in case it gets bad: *My name is Ben Cross. I am trying to get to Greeley, Colorado.* He also has the newspaper clipping that he has carried around since it was printed, the one detailing the sentencing of Ray and the death of Rachel.

It's dusty in here, in this bedroom, in this Sears mail-order house that was built a hundred years ago and which he bought when he was thirty and thus he has lived here for forty or sixty or a longtime years. He picks up a picture of his father and sees how dusty it is, and so he wipes the frame on the front of a shirt. It cleans the glass but leaves a smudge of dirt on the gray wool.

That's what his brain reminds him of: dust. That's how he sees the world. There are sometimes small specks of dust and sometimes whole rooms of dust, and sometimes it blows away and he can see very well and other times it is so dusty that he doesn't even know what lies on the other side of the dust.

The dust just needs some water.

But he cannot get enough water into his brain. He has to hurry. When you reach out to catch a chicken or a calf, you have to move fast, otherwise you end up just chasing. Fast movement is what is called for. No flinching.

He is afraid, yes. He has said his prayers. He has courage.

He hears a commotion coming from the front door of the house and so puts the picture back and puts the suitcase under his bed. He wonders if his parents will be waiting for him on the other side. He doesn't know who is out there, in the kitchen, but a dog is barking. Probably it is that gold-colored dog that doesn't bring back anything, even though it should.

He combs his hair in the bathroom. He says to the mirror, "Body is great, mind isn't what it used to be." People at the grocery or post office sometimes ask how he's doing. Sometimes he complains about his hip that hurts or his tooth that still aches even though the dentist did that thing that kings wear on their heads. But he cannot really say the big thing because there are no words. This is horrible, that he will die twice. "Stand with it," he says to the mirror. "You just gotta stand with it."

When he gets to the kitchen, he sees that it's Del, who is married to Carolyn. And Anton the sheriff. Both used to have Western-style mustaches; Ben remembers that. But now they are clean-shaven. Del with his sandy wavy hair. And Anton that has deep brown eyes and very deep brown hair, and for this reason this sheriff reminds him of Ray, the man who killed his daughter.

Del says, "Morning, Ben. It's me, Del, and Anton come to see you."

He shakes both men's hands, although Del hugs him anyway. When he's asked, Ben says, "The body's doing fine, but the brain's not so good these days," to which the men nod and say, "Doesn't that beat all?" and "I know it, and it's no good."

Ben is worried about the sheriff. Why is he here? Does he know something? But Anton is turned around, helping himself to a cup of coffee from the coffeepot. Next to the sheriff is the kitchen window, outside of which are the aspen trees, and he considers for a moment the white beauty of their trunks, and wonders how long until they will leaf out. Ben says, "Just stopping by for a visit, are you?"

"Yup. Dropping Satchmo off. Appreciate you watching her while we go on vacation. And Anton wanted to walk the place. Look for good fishing holes along the river, for when spring comes. We're thinking of walking out to the back. Want to join us?"

Not once has the sheriff walked out back, although Del has plenty of times. Del belongs to this place almost as much as Ben, coming over to help put up hay and fish and fix fence. He has put hours in on this place, to be sure. He is part of the family. It's fine if they walk the place.

Renny walks in the porch door then, huffing and grumbling, a frozen chicken in her hand. "Fred died," she says, holding the chicken out, upside down by the feet. "She didn't get put in last night. She was caught in the wire of the fence and froze."

Ben can tell she's angry and he's sorry about Fred, whom they have had for a long time. Fred has been a good layer; lots of double-yolkers. There is nothing to say. He thought the chickens were in when he locked their door. It's their job, really, to be in by dusk. He wishes he could hold Renny. Hold her and hold her and apologize and apologize. She throws the dead frozen chicken in the trash, considers it, and then pulls it out and sets it on the kitchen counter. He knows she's fighting tears and also wondering whether it's worth cooking; not really, since the work involved is far more than driving to the store and paying a few dollars for one already set to go.

Ben watches all the men, arms folded and legs spread, rocking back on their heels, as they watch Renny eye the chicken. He watches her too. Watches her scowl at it as she says, "There's some cinnamon rolls in that tinfoil. What's Jess up to?"

"Full," says one, and "Thanks, but no," says the other, and then adds, "Sorry about the chicken. It's always something. Jess is riding her horse. From our house here, actually."

"Isn't she supposed to be doing her homeschool work? Does she actually ever *do* anything? Shouldn't she be doing something useful?"

Del smiles at Renny, calm as ever. "She is. She's riding her horse."

Ben sits down in the kitchen chair. Renny faces him. "Well, we might as well tell him." Renny nods from Del to Ben. "Ben, I know this is complicated, and it's hard to understand. But you might remember us talking about it. Del and Carolyn are too cash-poor to buy this ranch, and besides, if they bought it outright, we'd have to pay capital gains taxes and that could kill us. Del and Anton have a new plan. They'll put a conservation easement on the place, which means Del and Carolyn can buy the land for its agricultural value. Not its commercial value. But one strip of land, over by the county road, we'll sell to Anton, who will buy that for development. He'll buy it from Carolyn and Del, which gives them the money to pay us. And lord knows we'll need the money for these years ahead. Okay?"

Ben feels hot and he looks around for the source. He will not let this ranch be sold to pay for his care. He will not gut this ranch like a fish.

Anton raises his coffee cup halfway to his mouth. "I think that plan honors your work here, Ben. A few houses on the south side, but the rest conserved. Everyone wants to do right by you. And of course, you two keep living here as long as you want to."

Renny walks up to Ben and so he is forced to stare at her. "If we die, Ben—if we suddenly die—Carolyn and Del will lose this place. Estate taxes. We need to sign the papers now, even if we plan on staying."

It is too hard, this crush-crush that goes on in his heart. Surely he knew he would not live here one day. Surely he had prepared himself for that? Surely he had known that the orange willow branches and the bald eagle, that all of it would pass to someone else? He doesn't remember. He doesn't remember considering it. There's no remembering in his brain. "Not those branches," he says.

The three of them regard him silently.

So he tries again. "Not the orange branches."

Again, they are silent, until Renny says, "Oh, the *willows?*"

"Willows," he says.

Del and Anton regard each other until Del says, "You're wanting us to leave the willows? They're farther north than Anthon wants to build anyway."

"I'll leave the willows," Anton says. "Sure. I'm thinking of putting five houses along the county road. Sell the lots to rich people who want to live out here in the country. But not big ugly houses—nice regular-people ones. That's not even near the willows, is it?"

Ben clears his throat. "I told Renny already, I'd like to be . . . that thing, when you are put into the ground—buried— here. She'll make arrangements with the county. Right Renny? Won't you?"

"That's a long way off, no need to be thinking of that—"

"No, he's right to talk about it." Renny gazes directly in his eyes. "We'll bury you here, Ben."

Then he watches Renny's sea-green eyes go soft, blink, sees how she folds for a moment into a sadness. She reaches out to straighten Ben's glasses, brushes her fingers along his temple as she does so. "We're heading into town to visit Rachel's grave. Today was her birthday. Are you ready Ben?"

Ben's tongue won't work and his mouth hangs open and he has a sense of a hope, some words floating in his brain, something about how he hopes she can catch his eyes too and will understand the truer part of him, will understand what he must do and why.

But now Del is clearing his throat. "Carolyn and Jess went over there this morning."

"It's the hardest thing," Anton says quietly. "I've got a funeral to attend in town myself today. The grandmother of one of the deputies."

Renny gathers her down jacket, ripped from barbed wire and stained with manure, and her purse, the same leather one she has had for years, and the dead chicken. She turns to Anton. "I'm sorry to hear that. About the grandmother. I hope she went quick?"

"No, actually, she didn't." He glances around the kitchen, then rests his eyes on her. "Cancer. This dying business isn't easy. Seems like when it's drawn out . . . Seems like with animals we do a better job. Seems like we haven't figured out how to do this right in this regard, when it comes to our own dying."

Ben looks past them, out the window, and that dog is trying to play with the chickens and they stare at him in response. He clears his throat. "My body's doing great, but my mind isn't what it used to be. Still, I know that the irrigation ditches need to be . . . cleaned up. The fence posts are . . ."

"Rotting?"

"Yes, rotting."

"Yes." Del scratches his jawbone. "I know. Carolyn told me you were concerned about them. I know what needs to be done. I could sure use your help, though. Always. Always, I could use your help."

"You're committing your lives to a certain hell," says Renny, who is telling the truth and making a joke, Ben knows. He knows Renny means that she considered living on this ranch like a hell, even as it was a heaven. And because their ranch's name, for a long time, has been Hell's Bottom Ranch, since they bought the place the year they were married, and the first time they had walked the place there had been a flood on the river and stuff was scattered everywhere and Renny had said, *It looks like the bottom of hell.* But she didn't mean it. Because even in that mess, it was heaven. They fell in love with each other and with this valley below the foothills of the Rocky Mountains. *Hell's Bottom, Colorado, that's where we live.* That's what Renny used to say. And Ben used to joke that it was named for the place from whence Renny came, her being so ornery and all. And she would joke that it was where she was going. Renny liked being known as a tough woman. Most women did, he supposed. She liked being the type of person who was a little hell swirled in with heaven. She used to say, *Ornery enough to keep everyone on edge, intriguing enough to keep them around.*

Now she says, "Ben, you ready? We're stopping by Rachel's grave, okay? I'll throw Fred out the window on the way. Save the fox from going to the trouble."

"I could use a bite to eat," he says, and she hands him a cinnamon roll. He wishes she would make him two eggs, because he does not like sweet breakfasts such as cinnamon rolls; he prefers two eggs scrambled up on top of a piece of buttered toast.

The dog, he sees from the window, is sitting in the snow, staring at a chicken that is *bok-bokking* at it. The dog scratches her ear. And now the chicken cocks her head at the dog. He thinks of his own mother and father, their sugar beets and their onions and their cattle. His parents were busy, always busy, and they didn't have too much time to give him attention, but they were good, and he misses them. He liked to go visit their graves, back when he could drive, because it made him feel that perhaps they were on the same spinning planet as he, and he seeing their graves helped him feel less alone.

He should have told someone how much he missed Rachel. That his heart ached and ached and even after he asked it to stop aching it ached anyway. He never spoke it and it ruined his mind. He could not forget his daughter, even though he wanted to. He remembers thinking, *We don't have memories, they have us.* Perhaps if he could have spoken, his brain would not have rotted.

He takes the glass of milk Renny is handing him. "Oh," he says, remembering something very important. And he wants so badly to go write it down. When he gets a moment to himself, he will write a list:

Tell Carolyn good-bye
Tell Renny good-bye
Tell willows good-bye
Tell ranch good-bye
Tell grandkids good-bye

Especially Jess, he thinks. He's always loved her extra-much, as she used to say when she was young. Extra-much.

He needs to speak it. He needs to hurry. Today, he will visit the grave of his daughter. He will put his plan into motion. He will tell everyone good-bye. He repeats it over and over, *Tell them good-bye,* so that he does not forget. He won't be cheated of that again.

RENNY

It seems it will never end. At the post office, from her PO box, she pulls a letter with a return address: *County Road EE, Greeley, Colorado*. Ray's scratchy handwriting, which she has not seen for more than a year now. Her heart skitter-scatters, just like his blue pen on white paper.

She rips open the letter. *Would like to come visit, would like to see you in person and apologize. Can certainly be in the presence of a police officer.* She scans the phrases quickly. *Legal. Earned time, automatic deductions, parole eligibility date. Paid my dues. Visit? If you allow. May I?* She feels the volcano of anger rise from her stomach to her face. And a *P.S. Rachel's birthday was around now, wasn't it? Can't remember the exact date. Embarrassed that I can't remember. I'm sure that's hard on you.*

She throws the letter in the trash, thinks twice, picks it up. Throws it back again. What a bastard. Can't even remember the birthday of his wife, of the woman he killed. February 16. February 16. February 16! Renny stands there, staring at the trash bin, trying to get the upper hand on her heart, which is racing now, racing. She's going to have one of those panic attacks, those horrible things she had after Rachel died, and so she stands there, breathing, *in out in out, calm calm.*

Her hatred of Ray doesn't need to go away, she decides. No, that she can keep. Because it's justified and appropriate. Damn-for-hell. Enough is enough. *I've had it. I've goddamn had it.*

The ding of the post office door rouses her. A rancher walks in—she doesn't know him, but he tips his cowboy hat, as he always does. Ruben the vet is right behind him, handsome as ever, liquid brown eyes and still the smile of youth, beat-up ball cap that he also tips, and she manages to smile at him.

"Hey, Renny." Ruben holds up his PO box key and tips it in a hello to her. She looks from his face to the rest of him, startled to see he's dressed in overalls splattered in blood. "Can I talk to you for a minute? It's important."

"Looks like you had a tough call today. Hang in there." She keeps moving. She knows exactly what this is about, the missing pink juice, and she can't deal with that.

He touches her shoulder. "Renny? I really need to ask you something important—"

She throws her arm out fast and sure, whacks him across the chest. "Step back, Ruben!"

"Whoa-now. Jeez, Renny."

She stares at him full on. She sees he is startled enough to have pulled himself up, shifted from the young man that he is into the fuller man he is becoming, and she realizes that this is precisely the time in his life when this upheaval is occurring, that this very moment and situation might be the tipping point.

"Goddamn Alzheimer's. If only I had some. And be particular about its influence. The memory of Rachel's death, for instance. I'd like to lose that one. Okay? Get the hell away from me, Ruben. I can't talk right now."

She pushes the door open and stands out in wide white world, blinking back tears. She sees herself, cooking for Ben, while he read to her from the newspaper. She remembers how she heard three blasts of Rachel's truck. How she glanced up, to look out the kitchen window. Irritated. Here was her daughter being loud and obnoxious once again. But then, something about the way Rachel jumped from her truck. The wave of her hair. How Rachel, running into the house, turned around and looked over her shoulder. How she must have seen Ray's truck pulling in the driveway. How Rachel burst through the door then. How Rachel was screaming, and Renny was so angry—god, weren't her daughters ever going to quit *needing* her with such ferocity?—and she started to yell at Rachel.

This is the moment that has become slowed down in her mind. Why didn't she lock the door, then? It would have taken three seconds. Three. If only she had done that. Because the next minute, Ray was in the door, raising a pistol, and Rachel was screaming, and there was blood everywhere. And Ben leapt up from his kitchen chair and ran after Ray, to tackle him, and Rachel was in her arms, dying. She had one small chance to save her daughter, and instead she yelled. And it takes everything she has not to yell now. To punch and scream and kick.

"Renny?" It's Ruben's quiet voice behind her.

She turns, breathes in. "Ruben, good to see you! I'm so sorry about that. I just . . . well. Haven't done that in a long time. We're late, Ben and I, to go visit Rachel's grave. Call me later, how about? I'll talk to you later. I really will." She says this while she walks to her truck, the last bit from the driver's seat, and before he responds, she shuts the door.

She throws the mail on the dash, where it lands on top of Ben's already-faded pink Valentine's Day card. "Here we go, then," she says. "Here we go, then." She must calm down, and the best way to do that is to talk. "I wish you'd taken me to Mexico," she says. "Just once. One vacation that you planned for me."

Ben doesn't say anything, but looks down at his hands, rubs his fingers together.

Renny backs the truck out, nearly hitting white-haired Violet in her Cadillac, who is just pulling in the parking lot. Then she takes a right at the stop sign onto the highway that will take her into town. On the way, she throws still-frozen Fred out the window and watches the red-feathered chicken go careening through the air and land on the snow. "We're going to pick up some flowers and visit Rachel's grave. Okay? Got it? That's our plan."

"I could use a bite to eat," says Ben. "Mexico," he says later.

She says nothing. Otherwise she will spew out every real thought she has ever had. There is no well of patience left. It's dry. Today is Rachel's birthday; she would have been forty. The very least she can do today is be kind. She's got to get a hold of herself. She'll be kind for just a bit longer in honor of her daughter, who was, come down to it, probably a kind person. It's true Rachel didn't have her act together, it's true she dated horrible men and married a horrible man, it's true that she had two children sired by different men, and it's true that no one was ever clear on who those men were, but come right down to it, she was in fact a kind person, if she'd just had more time, it would have shone through, which is probably some-thing Renny forgot to mention to Rachel because she was too busy telling Rachel that Rachel didn't have her act together. She sighs. She remembers the few times she lost her temper—really lost her temper—and Rachel was usually the brunt of it. She's sorry and has been sorry and wonders if she will ever not be sorry.

"I could sure use a bite—"

She breathes in, deeply. Begs herself for a steady calm voice. "Remember, Ben. When we'd first walked the place? The year we were married?"

"The river had just flooded."

"Yes. All that junk everywhere. Branches and debris. A wallet. A cow's skull."

"A beat-up canoe. I kept that."

"No, you did not keep the canoe, Ben. We hauled it to the dump. With the old fence posts, rusted barbed wire. But remember? That's when I said, 'Looks like the bottom of hell,' but I didn't mean it. But you'd said, 'Hell's Bottom Ranch it is then. Our heaven.'"

"Yes."

"It's been a little of both, no?"

"Oh, sure," he says. "It sure has."

"I thought after Rachel died that I was as close to hell as I'd get. If that's not hell, I don't know what is." *Except this*, she almost says, but does not.

He doesn't seem to hear, and although she glances at him twice, she sees no sign that he has anything to say to this, if he has any response, if he has any emotion to a dead daughter and the aftermath that it caused. If only he could *hear* her, hear the important things, and respond, but instead, he says, finally, "When is Carolyn coming by next?"

Renny sighs. Someone, anyone, to tell these things to. That's all she wants. "She's in Mexico, Ben. Now we have their dog, and they're flying to Mexico. When they get back, we're all meeting with a lawyer. To transfer the ranch. Because we're going to die, Ben. Okay?" She's so tired of explaining things to a two-year-old in a grown man's body. "I wonder if she should get the test. For Alzheimer's. She says that if it's positive, her health insurance might kick her off. I guess there's not much she could do, anyway. I'm going to lose it, Ben. I know you don't know what I mean, but I'm going to lose it." At this, she looks sideways at Ben, searches his face. She realizes, with a start, that Ben has tears snaking down his face.

"She's gone?"

She turns back to the road, drives. The pressure of her sorrow is breaking her eardrums. It's breaking her heart. They drive through the ugly part of town—the strip malls, the Greyhound station, the used car lots.

Later, he says, "Carolyn left already. But Jess is here."

"Oh, Ben," she whispers. "I've sunk as low as I can get. All the sudden. Today," and then says, more loudly and firmly, "You knew that, Ben. That she was going to Mexico with Del. For a vacation. Isn't that nice, that they're smart enough to take a vacation? I think it's nice. They need something fun together. Jess is fine, old enough to stay alone. Billy is in Europe. Jack is in San Francisco, studying to be a lawyer. Leanne is at college. The dog is with us. Anton's taking care of the cattle."

"She took a trip," he says. "For ten days."

"Five days. Then they'll be back."

"Yes, she took a trip."

She can't help it, the desire to reach over and strangle him. It occurs to her now that one of her daughters was killed in an instant, bloody and terrible, in her own kitchen. The other could die slowly of a long disease, in the same kitchen.

She puts the idea out of her mind; she's too close to panic

and insanity to entertain any thoughts. Thinking of her daughters dying. Instead, she considers how tired she is. Maybe she should have her thyroid checked. Maybe she's got cancer. She's so tired of doing everything. She's so tired of no one noticing.

Esme says that the memories that get saved are those that had strong emotional connection, which is why it hurts her that he never talks about their wedding day, or the birth of their children. He talks of water and cows and onions. He must never have loved her at all. What a waste of both their lives.

She's going to try. She wants to say something about a new important thought she has had. How spirits go up, toward the sky, but souls go down, toward the earth and toward water. Water runs down because the earth pulls it that way. The soul wants to go down, too, and grow roots, run like a river. And that maybe death is like water running backward. Could that be?

She wonders, for the both of them, if they'll be brave enough to face it. They'll have no choice, of course, but it would be nice to know they could muster calm confidence and composure and a bit of spunk. *Use death as your advisor*, she heard once. In that way, you live well, and you die well. If you have practiced, you can relax into it, which is the way to go. Kicking and screaming and scared, that's the worst way; it's no good to try to avoid the unavoidable.

But how can she put words to that?

She can feel the heat from the truck blasting on her feet. It feels as if her feet are touching hell. She needs to find some sky, some kindness, some love.

BEN

Ben watches her place a sheaf or hay bale of flowers on the earth. He forgets what kind, but they are the best, and they're the color of a girl's soft cheeks. Skin-colored pink on the pure white snow, which will turn to water and be absorbed into the ground, into Rachel's bones.

"Carolyn and Jess were here," Renny says, and Ben sees that a little tear has come from the side of her eye. He knows why. Because he sees that someone has arranged river rocks in a wave pattern on top of the snow, as if the river rocks themselves were a river. Cairns have been made too. Beautiful rocks from the river at the ranch. It was Carolyn and Jess who came to do that, to make a river of stones and mountains of stones, and it's these things that are making Renny cry.

He puts his arm on her shoulder and she says "Oh, Ben, today it's too much," and leans a little, but not completely, into him. Oh. He hasn't felt her do that in so long.

What is the word that says so much?

She says, "Today I can't . . . Today I need a . . ."

And he opens his mouth. What is the word? Maybe if he can singsong it?

"I just am all out . . ." And now she is sobbing, and it reminds him that she rarely cried in all their marriage, but when she did, it was loud horrible scenes, a sudden release of crashing energy.

He says, "I'm sorry I'm so sorry I am so sorry."

That's the word, that's the word!

She looks at him. Has he said those words before? No? Why does she look so surprised? He says them over and over until his brain is cleared out. He holds her to him and says it. Renny is crying and crying and crying into his chest. The dust has been blown away. He knows it's the right thing to say. The tip of his tongue grew back for just this one moment. To say he's sorry that this daughter is dead, and that his brain is dying, and that he couldn't stop either.

She stops crying and simply breathes into his coat jacket, right at the place it reads CARHARTT. He can feel the rise and fall of her lungs, how the breath calms and evens. She is nodding to herself, accepting his apology.

A bloom or gust of a feeling sweeps him. No words for it anyway. No words needed. Oh, Renny. He holds her closer to him. With a desire to be the *one* for her. Just like their first date. When they were young and giddy and had left a dance to drive up to see the lights from the top of the dam. How they got out of the pickup to look down at the town, the foothills all around them, and he pulled her suddenly to him, violent almost, not out of sexual desire but the other kind. To simply be perfect and whole together. The universe and love and these two particular souls named Ben and Renny. A fire burned up through their spines and was a huge energy that sprouted up and soaked the entire universe. For as long as the hug lasted. Everything made sense. Had a name and no name. The most complete moment of his life.

He rocks her back and forth, back and forth, and she holds him just as tight. But they cannot stay that way forever, and there's something he wants to say before the dust comes back, so he says it: "Renny, there's something to say before . . ." He pushes his lips into an *O*, so as to form a word. He can feel his body shaking, a small tremor, the tremor of age and effort, and he hates it. He wants to say: *I think you are the only person on the earth who will understand what I am going to do. I think you will be proud of me. I think I'll do right by everybody. I say good-bye to you. I say good-bye to the real you. The one that lives under your white hair and your familiar face. The real and true you that resides underneath the skin. The you I loved. On that night with the lights of the town and the lights of the stars.* But none of those words will grow on his tongue. So he says, "Renny—" and then there is a long silence.

Renny finally hiccups again and touches his arm. "I think I know, Ben."

"It's all right?"

"It's all right."

"And so."

"Yes."

"It's her birthday today."

"Yes."

"Well then. After lunch I need a nap."

"Yes, Ben. You always take a nap."

"They make me feel better."

"I know it. Ben? Were you ever lonely?"

He pauses. "Maybe I quit thinking about it. Off my radar screen."

71

"So it got better?"

When he doesn't answer, she says to herself, "I never did. Learn to quit thinking about the lonely. But I did start to live more narrowly. Occupying myself with other things. Instead of the big things. Like living well. And deeply. And being passionate about something. And being vital. Ben? Ray wrote us a letter. Today. He wants to come visit."

"I could use a bite—"

She bows her head. "Let's go get a bite to eat, then." She takes his hand—she's holding his hand!—and they leave the pink flowers and the smooth river rocks and the snow in this garden of stones.

But the dust blows back in. The dust of the dead. So he says to himself: *My name is Ben Cross and I am seventy-six and I have been a rancher all my life although now I own no cattle. Instead I have a disease in my brain. I own twelve hundred acres of pastureland below the Rocky Mountains and the snow remembers what it's like to be water. One night I held this woman and it was love, and our lives on the ranch were heaven. There is a man who wrote a letter.*

On the way back to the truck, Renny pauses, looks to the right, and points for him to see. It takes him a moment to find what she's looking at. It's a funeral up ahead at the other end of the cemetery. The sky is starting to spit snow on a group of people, on the far end, but even from here, he can see Anton step from the sheriff's cruiser. But wait. It's not Anton, it's Ray. Maybe it is Ray? The man who wrote a letter? He stops, startled. Sees a dark head, sees the wide shoulders and thick stance of a man.

He finds that his voice is quiet but then rising and soon yelling. His own voice is saying, "OH YOU, YOU . . . YOU—" His hands clench and he wants to be a boxer. "TELL YOU WHAT I'M GONNA DO SEE."

"Ben!" Renny touches his arm, looks off in the distance at the faraway funeral. "What the— Who are you— Why are you—? Ben! Settle down right now! I don't need *you* losing it."

"YOU MONSTER," he yells at Ray, across the cemetery, and starts to charge forward but trips and falls and stands back up. "I miss my—I miss my—my girl. My girl!"

"Knock it *off*, Ben. Now!" Renny stands in front of him and slaps him across the face. Even though it doesn't hurt he falls to his knees, right there in the snow. "What's wrong with you? They're having a funeral over there."

And still his voice is yelling, and still he is tumbling through the snow. "I'm sorry! You were never sorry. I'm sorry. You were never sorry!"

Renny is in front of him again, blocking him with her body. "Ben Cross!" She slaps him again, hard. "Stop!"

He sinks to his knees again. His voice says things on its own. "You put up a good front . . . all those letters . . . but under-neath . . . in that place . . . what place this is . . . that place? . . . in the core, in the middle in the silo in the center you are something, you are . . . something . . . sick and rotten."

"Oh, Ben. You're talking about Ray? Ben, settle down. That's not Ray over there. They're trying to have a funeral. Get in the truck." She is standing over him and she reaches down and grabs him under the armpit and pulls him up. She's so strong. She pulls him along, then she opens the door.

He must yell it to the garden of stones. "YOU FAKE. YOU ARE NOT HUMAN. YOU LACK COURAGE! COWARD COWARD COWARD!"

"Ben, Ben—Stop right now!" Renny is handing him a bit of toilet paper, dusty, so dusty. She has unrolled some from the roll they keep in the back seat. He realizes there is water. Water everywhere. Water pouring from his brain, down his face. All the water from his brain is pouring down his face. Down and down. Into the snow. He's losing his brain. He is leaking apart.

He remembers when the doctor said, *You have dementia, probably Alzheimer's,* and the doctor said it was important that he do two things. One was to get his will in order. The second was to make a list of all those things you "were going to do someday," and then put a star by the ones that made sense, that he *could* do, the ones that really mattered, like maybe a trip, or writing a letter, or making peace with a person, and to do them one by one, now, *do them now,* and it makes him weep because he didn't have too many things to put on that list—only one or two—and he realized then that his life had been too empty, he had grown too lazy, he had let life just *happen* to him, but there were a few things he listed:

Heal family
Protect ranch

And one more thing he had put two stars next to:

Ray

So he screams and screams at the cemetery and he turns around the other direction so that in the far distance he sees a blotch of pink throbbing from the snow. Then Anton is there, panting from the jog, holding him, one hand on each of his shoulders and saying "Whoa there, whoa there, buddy," as if Ben is a gone-crazy horse.

Anton and Renny are putting him in the truck. Bending his knees, making him sit. But his body has gone wooden and rigid and it takes a long time.

"I'm going to drive now," Renny says finally. "Anton is going to follow us home. Help me get you inside. I'll make you some eggs and toast. Oh, god," and then she is sobbing. "They said this would happen. That you'd start to lose your temper. Your personality would . . . change. For the worse. We just—we just . . . I thought we just had a moment that *mattered* . . . Oh, Ben—" and she looks at him, sorrowful and startled. "It's too late now?"

There are still screams in him that need to come out. But instead he cries with her. Even as he cries he knows Renny is driving and saying "Holy kamoly this is new oh no oh no I can't do this, not this" over and over and he can see that Anton is in the rearview mirror.

When they pull up into the driveway of their home, he sits in the truck gazing at the white farmhouse and barn and chicken house. He sits until Renny talks to Anton, and Anton leaves, and then she comes back to sit with him in the truck.

Renny puts her hand on his leg. He can feel how bony he is. He used to be so strong. She says, "Oh Ben. I wasn't aware that you . . . hated Ray so much—" Then she stops, tilts her head, says, "I think I know what you mean." And she says, "It's not that Ray was a monster, not outright evil. That's why, in certain ways, it's worse. Because he had the capacity to be a good man. People liked him. He had a certain charm. But deep inside, beneath those brown eyes, he was a fake and a bully. He didn't love her. He didn't love much of anything. And he was lazy and self-centered in about a hundred different ways."

Ben starts crying again because she is right. He can understand her, and she is right.

"We should have talked about this sooner. Why only now?" Renny nods as she says this, agreeing with herself. She pats him on the leg. "Listen. We're both worn out. I don't want you doing that, ever again. I don't know what's in store for us now, but not that. I don't know if you understand me. But it might be time—I'll think about it tomorrow—to move to that assisted care place. I can't . . . But for right now, I know what you mean, Ben. Rachel, for instance, saw enough in him to love. He had her fooled. With dreams of a piece of land. A future together. So it makes it worse, doesn't it? That when you look inside this supposedly good man, if you look hard enough, into his marrow, you can see that he was a pretend show."

"Pretend show."

"Yes. You're right, Ben. That's what he was. The difference between a real man and a pretend show is courage. Courage. Deep down he didn't have any. Isn't that right, Ben? Some people on this earth aren't even really human. And he was one of them. But he *looked* like the other kind—the good kind."

And Ben nods and cries and whispers words like *coward, go to hell,* and *all that.*

"Yes, all that." Later, she says, "It's getting cold out here, Ben. Let's go inside. Look at that snow. We're going to freeze to death in here. It would have been easier if he was evil. But no. He was just a fake. Everything except the gun was a fake. We should have told each other this sooner."

She leads him in the house, their footprints making new marks in a new snow.

On the way inside, she stops once. "Ben? If you were alive ten years from now, what would you want to be doing? Can you understand that question?"

He understands. Pauses to form the words of it. Only gets out, "Take care of you and the ranch." Or, at least, he hopes he says it. He doesn't look at her, though, to see her reaction. Instead he looks at the aspen trees standing in their winter silence, and the snow behind them is an octave whiter than the aspens themselves. Suddenly, he remembers how rain falls and the drops are held in the center of aspen leaves, how their circular perfection is held inside a cupped palm of leaf, and his heart snaps with the knowledge he won't see spring again. "Oh," he says, clutching at his heart. "It hurts. I'm scared."

Renny doesn't hear him, though, and once inside, she tells him to take a nap. But no, he says, he won't. First, he says, she must dial the number to his daughter's house.

Renny sighs but dials Carolyn's number and says, "The answering machine will pick up. Or Jess will. Although she never does. They're in Mexico. They're trying to do what we failed at doing, for a while at least. Keeping love alive through the tough spots. When it beeps, leave a message. Tell her whatever it is that you want to tell her." Her voice is kind, like the touches she used to give him. She holds the phone out and he holds it to his ear and waits for the beep.

Phones are difficult. He can't see the person's expression and so the words just smear around. But this will be okay, because it is his only choice. He hears his daughter's voice, not the voice she was as a girl but something that sounds very close to it, and then he hears a pause, he hears a beep. "Tell ya what I'm gonna do, see," he says into her answering machine. "I'm gonna tell you I love you. Good-bye, now. Carolyn. Jack, Leanne, Billy, Jess, Del, Carolyn. Tell ya what I'm gonna do, see. Love to you all." His voice gets very quiet, as if turned down on its own.

RENNY

The bravest thing she can do is to let him be. She wards
off the fear by doing the chores herself and doing them early
and well. She'll stay out of the house as long as she can. She
breaks the ice on the water tanks with a tamping bar, throws
hay to the donkeys and horses, fills her pockets with the dried
apple slices she made herself in the summer (she remembers
the smell of her sweat and the way the bees and wasps buzzed
around her as she sat outside cutting apples and putting them
on cookie sheets to dry). The horses nuzzle them softly from
her shaking hand, their eyes darkened with gratitude. The hens
are all huddled in the chicken house early, and she sends the
ice from their drinking pans shattering outside on the ground
before refilling them. She wipes the tears streaming down her
face continually, and something about this makes her think of
her DNA, of how hers falls into trampled hay, or into dirt, or
into snow, or onto an apple that gets eaten by a horse and how
she is now a part of that horse literally, which somehow makes

her less alone because she is binding with bits of the universe, and so is Ben, at this very moment.

She can see Jess has been there again. There's a pile of fresh horse manure by the barn and tracks in the snow—her own horses could not have made those tracks, penned in as they are. Renny glances around, but there is no sign of her now. She could use Jess right about now. Funny, she decides, how important it is, simply having another breathing living human next to you during heart-slashing times. Even if you don't talk.

Though she has not walked out back in months, despite the dropping temperature and spitting snow and lowering sun— despite all this—she takes a walk now. She is so cold. She is so tired. She must stay out of the house, because then the decision will have been made. It will be over. It's an act of cowardice and bravery at the same time.

Satchmo follows her, rolling and pouncing on wind-swept snowdrifts and yet somehow obedient, as if she knows that Renny is close to a certain line that should not be crossed. The dog comes jogging up to Renny sometimes and snuffles her hand with a nose, and Renny relents finally and pets her head with her gloved hand and despite herself finds herself mumbling things like *Okay, you stupid dog, okay, don't worry, your family will be home soon.*

She wonders if she should run home and call someone. Perhaps Eddie, Ben's oldest friend. Perhaps Ruben, the vet. Perhaps Jess. But no: She will not burden them with this particular load. Only she could possibly understand. Only she could love Ben enough to give him the freedom.

At Ben's cabin, she pulls off the leather work gloves and lets herself in the door. The silence feels as if it could nearly burst her eardrums apart. It's cold, very cold, and she can see the breath misting in front of her in clouds that dissipate and appear, dissipate and appear. There is a simple fireplace along one wall, and it sits empty and dark, mocking her with the lack of heat that it could provide, a simple case of matches and dried wood, and this unfulfilled possibility reminds her of herself, where there's not a flicker of light or barely one at all and she wonders, yet again, if she should go to a doctor herself and ask for antidepressants or antianxiety pills or something, which she never in a million years would have thought were necessary, given her energy and spirit and spunk, but which Carolyn suggests over and over, and which now she will no doubt need. "Oh god," she says to the empty fireplace. "Oh please god. Take him kindly."

The dog has been trotting around, sniffing, wagging, but comes up to her at the sound of her voice. "Stupid dog," she says, but reaches down to pet her. "Ben liked it here."

She remembers well the contentment that swarmed around him after this cabin was built. A sad mourning contentment, but contentment nonetheless. Unlike the crowded dusty farmhouse, cluttered with doilies and knickknacks and years of kids and grandkid photos, and of their artwork, and of presents given, of accumulated debris, of a messy but full life, everything here is simple, clean, tidy. In that way, it seemed fake to her. A mirage. But it's built sturdy, and lets in less dust. And perhaps there is nothing wrong with a mirage from time to time.

She herself was relieved to be alone during that time. At least, at first. She could move through her days—the grief-filled ones and the slightly better ones—at her own pace in her own way. It was a gift, she decided, to live alone in a house. But the heart can house many emotions at once, and she was also angry at him for leaving. Lonely when she ate dinner. Bitter about the farmwork and how there was so much of it, even though they continued to share it. Plus, she was cold at night, with no body heat. And ultimately, this life was boring. Or something that resembled boring. She missed the chaos of life—the full catastrophe of living, as she called it, a phrase she lifted from *Zorba the Greek*. She was not *in* her life, not really living it. She was living a small life, and that seemed a crime.

She walks into the bedroom. Ben had slept on a single mattress and frame that he had taken from Carolyn's old bedroom. The comforter, flowered and also from the same bed, is tidily arranged. He had also moved in Carolyn's old dresser, handmade and wooden and simple. She opens the drawers. There are white handkerchiefs, undershirts with stained armpits (and she knows that he didn't shop for things such as packages of undershirts once they had split up; he probably didn't even know how). In the next drawer down is a pair of jeans, two work shirts. More slips of paper—always bits of paper—which she unfolds. There is her name, the names of the neighbors, instructions on how to play bridge (Oh, how smart he had been!). Always in pencil. She leaves them there, all of them. She looks in the closet and there are only shoes, all old ones, including a pair of slippers she had once given him in the very early years of their marriage. She remembers shopping for them, picking out the best pair of soft leather with sheep wool inside. Back then, she had truly loved him, truly wanted his feet to be warm and protected. She remembers clearly standing at the store, holding them, debating whether they were worth the price, and she had been filled with a wave—yes, that was the right word—of gratitude for having Ben and her daughters and a ranch and the emotion called love lodged in her heart.

There is one time in her marriage that stands out. Like the first kiss, it was the one other time when she felt as if time stopped, when the world made sense, when the love was so evident and pure that it contained all of time *in* it. They'd been working cattle, all of them, except Rachel, who had already died. Carolyn had been explaining to Jess, who was newly moved in with her, about prolapses and how the best thing to do was to shove the uterus back in and sew the cow up with thick string and give her a shot of penicillin. Jack had been trying to gross Jess out, in a teasing way, and was telling her how heavy and slick the uterus was, how it took two people, one to hold the uterus up, one to push it back inside the cow. Then Ben and Jack had gotten busy with running the cattle through, sometimes arguing about which bull's semen to use next year. Leanne was taking notes and Billy was quietly sitting in a corner, and the cattle were bawling and banging around the corral and it seemed like a particular, wonderful moment.

But inside this particular, wonderful moment were the specific details that made it so. How, for example, Ben was scratching a yearling heifer on the hump between her ears, and when the animal raised her head to sniff his shirt, she left a smudge of mucus on his sleeve, which Ben eyed in an offhand way and then he leaned over, during the height of the argument about bull semen, and rubbed it on Jack's face. Which caused Jack to fling it off back onto Ben, and then Jack punched Ben and Ben punched Jack, in a good-natured fond way, which made Billy giggle—it was the first sound anyone had heard from Billy in a long while—and which made everyone smile.

Inside this moment were the cattle, pressed against the railing to eye the two boxing men, watching with sleepy interest, flicking their tails against the flies.

Inside this moment was Leanne, sitting on the cement rim of the stock tank, in shorts and sandals and with a clipboard on her lap, keeping records. Jess went to sit next to her, to learn the ropes, to become the family's new record keeper.

Inside this moment were the details, such as the words being thrown into the air: *X-1-5-1. Polled. 595 pounds. Ninety days pregnant, I reckon.* Details of the routine. How every year, the cycle started. Pregnancy-checking, then calving season, then moving the cattle to spring pastures, then haying, then weaning, then castrating, then pregnancy-checking again. Some of the cattle were sent to the sale barn or to slaughter. Some were kept. Some were sold. And in that moment were all the years that had layered up and woven together; all the turquoise skies and all the cottonwoods dropping golden leaves. All the calves being born, slipping from their mothers. All the times one of them had flapped their arms to move the cattle into the alleyway that led to the chute. All the shoulder-length latex gloves being put on, the hand being reached into the cows to feel unborn babies. All the times on the horses, rounding up the calves. All the sun and sky and smells. All the warm fall days and the summers and the winters. And how, on that one day, it was all enough, held together in one moment, and it was enough to hold her heart together.

She shakes her head, like a horse, and comes out of her daze. "I guess I'll try to think of that moment when I die, Satchmo. That and the first kiss and today at the cemetery." When she says this, the dog picks up a slipper in her mouth and trots off into another room. Inviting her in. Indeed, when Ben is gone, after tonight, perhaps she can move back here. She'll tell Carolyn and Del to leave her alone and she'll leave them alone. The grandkids can visit, but she won't insist. She'll not worry about the state of Carolyn and Del's finances or marriage; about whether or not Jack is gay, because he is and it's time she loved that about him; about whether Leanne will become a silly language arts major and therefore never be able to support herself; whether Billy will ever do anything with his life other than ranchwork;

whether Jess will end up like her mother, pregnant, drinking, on drugs, and dead too soon. No, she'll just let them conduct their symphony, their own lives. She'll go out to town twice a week to grocery shop and see a movie, maybe with Zach. Otherwise she will sit and rest and rest and rest. And by god, she'll appreciate that no one, nothing, is depending on her, which will mean the first time in fifty years—or possibly forever—that she will be her own person. Of course, she realizes, this will also be very lonely. And then she will die. And like every human, she should brace for it. For all she knows, death could happen for *her* tonight.

Satchmo nuzzles the sleeve of Renny's jacket and so she says, "You got that right. I don't think I want to move into town after all. If I live in a condo, I'll have to listen to babies cry and dogs bark and other people. Horrible."

The dog whines, more insistent, and licks her hand.

"Okay, we'll go. I'm just trying to figure out what to *do*. You can visit me back here, but only if you're quiet and respectful."

On her way out, she stops again in the main room, and from this angle she can see the corner not visible from the door. There is a deck of cards scattered on the floor. She stares at it and then registers the folded-up sleeping bag tucked back between the wall and couch. There's also a pillow, backpack, a cardboard box with a few items, such as tampons, and she understands Jess has been sleeping here.

"Huh." She says it aloud, surprised, then says it again. Well, good: At least the cabin is getting some use.

Life, she once heard, is the combination of two things: Certain points of interest, which stand out. And the flux of experience, which is one big blending of time and space. And they come together to form the important stories and moments in your mind. The stories that define you. She reckons that that's how folks survive the ache of it all.

On her walk back across the ranch the sky turns to a dusky blue and reflects a lighter blue off the blue landscape and the snow picks up the blue again. The dog races ahead, toward home, leaving her alone with the expanse of blue snow to either side. Walking is hard out here, although she follows Ben's track that he's worn down. She sees what he has always seen, the sheer beauty of the place in twilight, the shadow of willows and foothills and cottonwoods along the river. A dark figure—probably a bald eagle, she figures—sits on a branch far to the north. She is simply not sure what should come next for Renny Cross. Although she knows that tonight everything will change and that it's high time she thought about it.

Ben's screaming and hollering, and her understanding of what he is grappling with now, has worn her out. It is such a deep exhaustion that it borders on peace—a dictated and unavoidable peace, she thinks. She wonders if she should have told Ben more about Ray's letter that came today, but no, he would have felt the same way: that it was simply not enough. It was adding insult to injury. It makes her sick. Sick that Ray is out of prison, sick that he offers these little tiny bits of effort, sick that he didn't remember Rachel's birthday, not because she wants him to know a particular date, but because she wants him to know the *details* of Rachel. He knew only what he wanted to know. Ray only wants his conscience off his back, but no, she won't allow that. And Ben wouldn't want it either.

At home, she stamps her feet to warm up and starts up the woodstove. She wipes the tears from her eyes. She feeds Satchmo dry dog food and makes Tuna Helper and frozen peas for herself. Pitiful. She leaves Ben's plate in the microwave and goes to watch the news. Mainly, though, she is shaking—a real tremor—and she watches the new snow come down outside the window, lit up by the outdoor barn light. Then suddenly it is really starting to snow, now, and the bottom of the TV screen warns of a blizzard. She starts to sob-cry and she considers calling someone, just to talk, but she's not sure who, and in any case, she would need an excuse—to report a cow on the road or ask if anyone has chickens for sale—because she's never called anyone without a pretense for calling. She has no friends. She breathes out and considers this room in the old farmhouse, big and open and yet dark and full of plaster cracks.

At that moment, the phone rings. She startles. Maybe it's Violet or some other local checking in, or maybe it's Zach or Esme from the Alzheimer's crowd, or maybe it's Carolyn or Jack or Leanne or Jess or Billy, and she is thinking of these possibilities as she jumps for the phone and picks it up.

"Renny, it's Ruben," she hears, and she winces. The one person she didn't want to talk to.

"Why, Ruben. I'm just watching the news—"

"Did Del and Carolyn get off okay?"

"Yes, yes. And we've got their stupid dog and—"

"Jess is okay?"

"I guess. She's off in her own world and—"

"Well, good. That's good. Listen, Renny. I have a question for you. When I came over last week to put down Don Quixote—and I'm sorry about that, I sure am—my sodium pentobarbital went missing. We vets call it pink juice. It's what I use to put down the animals."

"Oh, Ruben. We've been ranchers long enough to know about pink juice."

"Well you know, then, that it's a controlled substance. I have to account for every cc of it that I use."

"Oh, I'm sure you do. Dangerous stuff."

"Yes, yes, in fact it is."

"And it's gone missing, you say?"

"I had the bottle out, I remember, as we were kneeling around the donkey. I had it propped on a stick in the pasture, on the snow. I remember withdrawing the pink juice into the syringe, and I thought I put the bottle back in my bag. My black bag. I remember . . . injecting the donkey, I remember listening for the donkey's heartbeat. I remember chatting with you two. And then I remember leaving. But I don't have that bottle now. I just don't. I don't remember what I did with the bottle."

"Poor Don Quixote," Renny says. "You know, even when Billy and Jess were young teens, they used to ride that donkey all over the ranch. They just doted on that sweet girl. She was way nicer than Norm. Norm was a bully. Norm was the only donkey we ever had that I didn't like, and that's because his soul was mean—"

"I know it, I remember him. Listen—"

"Of course, the best donkey we ever had was—"

"Yes, but Renny, I hate to ask this, I'm so embarrassed, but I simply don't know what happened to that bottle. I'm wondering if you've found it, or if you think maybe one of you picked it up and put it somewhere. I took the liberty of stopping by your place today. After I saw you at the post office. You and Ben were gone, but I figured you wouldn't mind me looking around. Her . . . carcass is there, still . . . the animals have . . . well, that doesn't matter. I walked that back pasture back and forth. No sign of the bottle, though."

"I haven't been out there myself," Renny says. "Not since you put her down. Of course, that's why we put her down way back there, because no one *goes* there—"

"I didn't go into the house, of course."

"Well, it's not inside the house."

"Well, I'm just wondering . . ."

Ruben pauses and for a moment Renny wants to tell him the truth, wants to blurt out everything, only she is completely frozen, she cannot, she will not, because she believes that the pink juice exists for putting animals out of suffering, and Ben deserves that. She purses her lips in order to keep them shut. The tears leak out, though; those she cannot stop. Finally she says, "Ben didn't mention anything. He sure didn't. I'll ask him, but he's sleeping right now. If you don't mind waiting till tomorrow. If you wish, you could come over and we could search the place together."

She waits. Finally Ruben clears his throat. "It's a big problem, you see. I could lose my license for this sort of thing. I've searched high and low. I've gone through my vet bag and I've gone through the back of the truck. I just don't understand how I could have forgotten to replace it. You don't think Ben has it, do you? Would you mind, uh, looking through his things? You wouldn't think that he . . ."

She feels so calm. Calmer than she has in years. Calm and quiet and at peace. She lets Ruben pause, and she tells him that she'll go look right now, that she'll search through Ben's things, and she ends the conversation with him. She stands by the phone for a long time, holding the receiver in her hand.

She knows she should go in and check on Ben. She knows what she will find.

Ben and the bottle and death.

She can't bear to break the peace until the last minute, because after that, there will be no peace, not for a long long time. Everything from casseroles to people pestering her endlessly to her grief. Finally, she puts down the receiver, looks around the silence of her living room, and walks slowly to the bedroom. She steadies herself on the doorframe, breathes in. She pauses, wills herself to be strong. Then she looks at the bed. "Oh, god," she says aloud. Because he is not there. Not dead, not alive. Ben is nowhere. There is nothing except the twilight-blue comforter that she pulled tight this morning.

"*When he shall die,*
Take him and cut him out in little stars,
And he will make the face of heaven so fine."

—WILLIAM SHAKESPEARE

Romeo and Juliet (act 3, scene 3)

BEN

The snow whirls and circles and makes Ben dizzy, but he loves looking outside the window of the bus anyway, because the snow seems so alive and so charged with energy, and because he likes to think of the molecules of water, frozen, that will unfold when the temperature is right. He's alone in his seat, and the bus is nearly empty, and he feels the strange sensation of excitement in his chest and closes his eyes to better feel it. He hasn't felt this way since he was a child. Or maybe, no, when he fell in love. During sex. Pure energy, pure joy.

Tonight is a good night. Is it wrong to be proud of a moment like this? He's done everything right. He left their truck in the driveway—the pink card he made Renny still on the dash—and instead he took the old brown Ford that rarely works and which was parked on the far side of the barn. He had the presence of mind to get his suitcase and wallet and Carhartt jacket and even steal the rest of Renny's money from her purse while she was out doing chores, and he waited until she was in the chicken house to pull out of the driveway. He had the presence of mind to park at a 7-Eleven and walk to the Greyhound station and buy a one-way ticket to Greeley, which cost $15. He had the presence of mind to pay for the ticket with a $100 bill and accept the change even though he wondered if he was supposed to leave a tip.

He sits now, with his suitcase on the floor and balanced between his knees and looks out the window. The seat is soft, a blue fabric. *Oh Ben, oh Ben,* he addresses himself, *you're doing it.* What a simple thing, but a grand thing!

He loves this night sky, when everything is merely shadow. It's snowing, snowing, snowing, and from the passing car lights he can see how the flakes toss in air currents. For a moment, he is startled to know he can't remember the name of the man he knows he's going to see. But then he tells himself not to worry because he will remember and besides he has written it down somewhere on a piece of paper, and so then, calmed, he watches the snow.

When the bus stops, he walks up to the driver and the driver says, "This is only Loveland, sir, and I think you're bound for Greeley," and so Ben turns around and finds his seat again. He feels that it is still warm from him sitting there before, and he appreciates the simple fact of blue cloth. He doesn't need to go to the bathroom and he isn't hungry, and he's happy to be left alone by his body and its needs. He can simply watch the snow. The bus is stopped for a long time, it seems to him. People are getting on and off, and cold air seeping in, and the wind is picking up and the snow is starting to fall heavy, and the driver is talking on the radio. But he can ignore all this, corral it into only a small corner of his mind, and instead just watch the storm.

When he faces forward, though, he finds that another man is sitting next to him and the man is saying, "Hope you don't mind, I like to sit near the front, otherwise I get sick," and Ben does mind, he glances around but it's true the bus has filled up. There's a woman-girl behind him that looks so much like his dead daughter that it startles him. He wonders, for a second, if she isn't really dead. That he has been mistaken.

"Luce," the man says, putting his hand out, and so Ben shakes it. "Where you heading?"

"Oh, that place," he says, and then to stall for time, he adds, "I didn't know so many people took a bus. You know that town? Out there on the . . . plains. Greeley."

"Greeley always smells."

"Yes, that's true."

"It's the slaughterhouse."

"Yes. But it's gone now." Ben thinks of the town on the plains, the town where he was born and where that bad man now lives, with its acres of land and old train depot. He has never heard of a man named Luce and wonders if that's his brain or simply a strange name. His granddaughter's name starts with the same letter, *L*. And his other granddaughter's name is a *J*. They are good kids. They will be fine. He tightens his knees around the suitcase and feels for his wallet, which he has put into the front pocket of his gray pants, and yes, it is there.

"So you got one of those bracelets, huh?" The man says this and it takes Ben some time to realize he is talking about Ben's safe return bracelet, so that he can be tracked like a cow, branded, returned to the right owner. Since Ben can't form any words he just shrugs. He hates being embarrassed.

"My dad had one of those." The man has pockmarks on his face, ugly ones, and teeth missing, and Ben feels sorry for a young man with a face like that.

"Oh?"

"Me and my dad never did talk much, so I never knew it until one Christmas my sister called and said that I better get home and say my good-bye while he could still remember me."

"Oh," says Ben. "Yes, I guess that's important. Good-byes are important."

"So I did. Though he was mean as ever, and I wish now I hadn't given him the pleasure of seeing me again." Luce glances up at the driver and pops a wad of chew into his mouth and offers the tin to Ben, who shakes his head, no. Ben wonders if he should sleep or instead listen, but he feels lonely, he feels alert, he misses talking just for the sake of getting to know a person. He wonders if strangers always talk this much, telling personal stories.

"My dad was and is an asshole. You know what? He's going to spend all the money he ever had. Jerk. Because money does help. Let's face it. He could buy some forgiveness with money, that's a fact. People don't want to admit to that truth, but it's true. By the time he finally dies, there won't be anything left."

"Yes. Oh, yes." Ben doesn't know for sure what to say. He feels so excited and happy, and he just wants to hang on to that. But he should be careful, he knows it. Maybe this man takes drugs and will rob him. So Ben has to be careful not to let the dust out. Not let the dust out of the corral.

The man unpacks a sandwich, a store-bought kind with meat and cheese, and suddenly Ben's stomach rumbles and the man tilts half the sandwich at him and Ben shouldn't take it, he really shouldn't, but he's so hungry, and his mouth just says, "If you don't mind, sure," and his hand is holding it. He should have remembered to pack food. "I'll pay you for it," he says, and reaches into his wallet, and the man objects but Ben is no taker of handouts and so he pulls out a bill and stares at it for

a long time to make sure that it is the right size of bill, it has a
1 and two *0*'s and that seems right for a sandwich, so he hands
it to the man and the man pauses and says, "Huh," and then,
"Well, thanks," and so Ben knows he's done a good job.

The sandwich is very good. He likes the feel of different tastes
and feelings in his mouth. He likes the snow coming down.

"You're doing all right, though? Traveling alone and all."
The man's food falls from his mouth and onto his lap, little bits
of lettuce and tomato.

"My body's doing great but my mind isn't what it used to
be. Although my arm is kind of feeling . . . something . . . I don't
have the word. I'm not as bad as some people who go to those
meetings, though. Can't complain."

"Well, good." The man opens up a bag of chips, which he
offers to Ben. "That's good."

"I came up with a new saying. Tell you what I'm gonna do,
see. I'm going to stay tuned in as long as I can." He remembers suddenly an earlier time, when he was a young boy, and
he came upon a heifer at his parents' ranch, and the heifer
was dead and swollen with bloat, and her two top legs were
sticking out in the air. She wasn't cut or bleeding or anything
that he could find, but when he walked around behind her, half
of a calf which was also dead was coming out her rear end,
and that was the first time he had seen what birth looked like
and what death looked like, all in one snapshot of an instant.
Something about that reminds him of why he is on the bus.

The man is chuckling like a bird. "Stay tuned in. I like that."

"Doesn't take long to kill things," Ben says. "Takes a lot
longer to *grow* things."

The man pauses and chews. "That's true, I guess."

Ben's mind wanders to a game he once played with his
grandchildren—he can't remember the name of it—but there

was an orange card that said GET OUT OF JAIL FREE. Then he finds his voice and his words. "Renny is my wife. I have a daughter and four grandchildren. And a ranch. Later the dust will get heavier. But not yet."

"You'll lose your signal."

"But not yet."

"I wonder what that's like." The man is itching his wrists, then picks at his face, then itches his wrists. "That sure must be strange. Hope you don't mind me asking."

"Oh, it's a strange thing," Ben says, and he wonders if the man has a disease, like the cows get, and needs some ointment for those wrists. "I think you can put it on pause. Like a movie. And it will freeze. Like those fields outside. Someday they will melt, but not now."

"You got that right," says the man. "Looks like we're going to get a downright blizzard."

For a long time they sit quietly, looking out, and Ben hides his bracelet under his shirt sleeve. It looks like the man with the ugly face and the missing teeth has closed his eyes, and perhaps fallen asleep, and Ben is glad for that. He loves the bus moving and the sound of Greeley coming closer and closer. Ray. That's who he's going to see, Ray. And there's a slip of paper in his pocket to remind him what to do.

And then, startling them out of the hush, the bus driver says on a loud thing, "I'm sorry to report, folks, that I-25 as well as the side roads have just been closed by the highway patrol. Up ahead is Ed's Place, and I'm stopping there."

Ben hears the people groan.

The man sitting next to him says, "Ah, fuck. I knew I should have left yesterday."

Ben wishes he had tied a string from his suitcase to his hand. He must not, he must not, he must not, he must not lose this thing. He tells himself over and over as he walks off the bus with his suitcase, behind the others, and underneath an orange neon sign and a huge sky blowing fast and angry flakes. He ducks his head and the snow is smacking his face, hard, and he follows the others inside and follows a few men into the restroom. He goes into a stall and takes a piss but then he sets the suitcase on the seat of the toilet and unbuckles the suitcase and takes out the bottle and the syringes. He tries to fit them in his sock but it's no good, they don't fit. Finally he puts them in his jacket, one that Renny bought him years ago, which has deep pockets. In the suitcase he leaves the gun tucked in with the clothes and the picture of Ray from the newspaper and the name of Ray and some other slips of paper. He can't remember if they are important or not. The gun is important as backup, because he's learned the hard way that you should always have backup, you should always be able to put an animal out of its suffering. At the last minute, he takes out one of the newspaper articles and folds it and puts it in his pocket. He makes sure he has everything before he leaves. He double-checks——*jacket, wallet, suitcase*—so that he will not forget these three important things.

He finds a booth and orders a piece of cherry pie from the waitress, who is chubby and young, but who he realizes is not chubby but has a baby growing inside her.

She says, "Well, looks like we're all stuck here for the night. At least we got food. Could be worse. Pie and coffee? That's all? Coming right up." When she returns with the pie and coffee and he decides to order a sandwich—just some sandwich, he says, he can't remember the name—and she regards him carefully and says, "That's the order I'd eat my food in too. Hamburger coming right up." He hopes that this woman has a baby girl.

"Join you?" Ben looks up to see a man, who is young, in his twenties, more of a boy than a man, with a *bok-bok* marked face, and some missing teeth, and not handsome at all, in fact, ugly.

"I'm Luce," says the man. "From the bus. I gave you some sandwich."

Ben is tired. His brain feels dummy and dusty. "Well, hi, Luce," he says. "I'll buy you dinner."

The man cocks his head at him. "That would be great, thanks. A man can always eat. Doesn't it smell good here?"

Ben can't smell anything and wonders, briefly, why he can't smell anything. He hasn't smelled anything in a long time, as if that part of his world has been erased. "That's the truth, a man can always eat."

"Yes, it is."

When his hamburger comes, he tries to smell it. There is nothing: only air. But it looks good and he feels his mouth water. The boy-man says, "So, does it piss you off? Make you bitter? I always wanted to ask my dad that, but he wasn't the talking type, plus now he wouldn't know what the hell I was talking about."

Ben wishes this boy would talk slower and not ask so many questions, but he says, "Yes. I just wish there weren't such a thing."

"You got that right. My mom died of cancer a long time ago. I used to wish that one day we'd wake up on this planet Earth and there would be no such thing as cancer, either."

"This planet could do without a lot of things."

"You got that right. Ticks, for one thing. I don't see the point of them. I sure as hell hate ticks."

Ben is so tired. He's scared, suddenly, because he knows he needs to sleep and there is no place to sleep. He is dizzy. He won't be able to do it. He waited too long. The rooms spins as if he has just stepped off an amusement ride. He is going to sleep, with his jacket on, his wallet in his pants, and his hand on his suitcase. He wants to say something, to this kid. He wants to say, he had many good years, yes. Years when he woke up and he was very happy with the world—and at the end of the day, he would go to sleep and still be happy with the world. He would wake next to Renny, and the canary would be singing from the laundry room and a donkey might bray or a cow might bawl. And when he did chores out back, the canyon wrens would sound by the river. Oh, he was happy. He was useful. He had a good life.

Except for one horrible thing that ruined it all, and that thing has a name. Ray.

RENNY

When Renny calls Anton and blurts out that Ben's missing and she's already checked the house and outbuildings, Anton gets up out of bed and dresses and drives through the night and snow. When he arrives, he does what she asks, which is to drive out back to check the cabin and the fields, just to make sure Ben hasn't wandered back to his favorite places. She could do that herself but she wants to stay near the house in case Ben is there, hiding, or if he comes in suddenly. There are so many crannies in a farmhouse, and on a farm, and she gets the flashlight and the dog and walks through the outbuildings again—the haystack, the shed where Jess hangs out, the corrals, the chickenhouse, the old root cellar—hollering Ben's name. It's freezing out and she wants a hot bath and she wants to go to sleep. But she is also jittery, and now that she doesn't know where Ben is, or whether he's alive, she feels like an electric wire. She sees her confusion like a huge gaping hole. She thought they had communicated with each other in the cemetery today. She thought she had understood.

She looks in the barn last, looks for the bottle and syringes. They are, as she predicted, gone. But where is Ben? She realizes he must have gone outside to do it, which makes sense. Better in the natural world, better to not leave a home with the stain of death. The kitchen, for instance, has never felt the same since Rachel died there. She understands, then, that they will find him frozen out in a field somewhere, looking up at the sky.

It's then, rounding the corner of the barn, on the way back to the house, that something catches her eye that she can't quite place until slowly it comes to her. The old brown Ford is missing.

This is unexpected: He hasn't driven for a long time. She's surprised that he would remember all the tiny steps that are taken for granted: the right key held steady and put into the right slot and turned in the right direction. Much less the right gear, the backing out, the driving away. It's the technical things he's had the most problems with. He can do uncomplicated things that require only one item: shovel the sidewalk, sweep the floor, dig in the irrigation ditch. But small fine-motor-skill things requiring many steps, no.

She stands in the snow, hands jammed into her jacket, and blinks at the empty space by the side of the barn, still stunned. She remembers when they first set eyes on each other: she from the mountains of Colorado, he from the plains, meeting at the college where they both studied agricultural sciences, and how the university building was a huge complicated mess—designed by a madman, no doubt—and she was lost on her first day of classes. She was as confused then as she is now. But she remembers how she turned a corner and ran into him, and how he helped her find her room, joking and bragging all the way that he had superior spatial orientation, and that he would be happy to help her any time—*any time*—she got lost.

He did indeed have an excellent sense of direction. Any time they went camping or hiking or on road trips, he was good at getting them off the usual trails and roads but then getting them back on. He was grounded and comfortable in the world. He knew his way around.

She shakes her head, coming to. A snowflake has landed directly in her eye and it stings for the moment it takes to melt. She runs inside, decides to call Ruben as she goes. When she explains, Ruben agrees to drive over to Carolyn's to see if Ben has, for some reason, gone over there. Ben had been so insistent on calling Carolyn, even though she was in Mexico—perhaps, she tells Ruben, he just didn't understand. Or maybe he wanted to check on Jess. Plus, it's the only home she figures he can still get to.

She wants to say the rest of the story, which is that she had thought he was going to kill himself—but how can she admit to or even give words to such a thing? And so she listens to Ruben's silence, his confusion, his starts and stops to questions; she knows he's wondering about the pink juice.

As soon as she hangs up, she calls Ben's old friend Eddie, and he agrees to drive around to the local spots—although all of them are closed—Violet's Grocery and Fern's Restaurant and the Swing Station Bar. He agrees to drive up and down the roads, looking. She can hear the warning in his voice—no one would last long out there in this snow.

And because Anton is still out back, still looking, she calls Esme, rousing her from a sleep that takes Esme some time to shake off—and Esme calls the police, who put out a bulletin, and within five minutes, unbelievably, the police call the house and tell her that the old brown Ford registered in Ben's name has been found in town at the 7-Eleven parking lot. It keeps surprising Renny: that Ben took the keys from the hook by the door and chose to drive all the way into town, obviously on purpose, obviously on the sly.

She does not call Carolyn, she does not call Leanne in Boulder, Jack in San Francisco, or Billy in Europe. She is shaking, now, from exhausted nerves; feels the vomit in her throat; and feels the dark blackness of the loneliness she has been beating back coming to blanket her and suck her away. She stands at the kitchen sink, hands braced there. The light at the top of the barn backlights the aspen trees. She does not, in fact, know where Ben is. That simple fact makes her want to freeze to the floor.

But there is no time for her to succumb to that. There is now a flurry of activity. Anton comes back, ice crystals on his face and eyelashes, stomping his feet and sending snow across her floor. When he hears the report of the missing truck, he promptly leaves for town. Eddie and Ruben hear the news too and drive into town to look around as well. And Renny, as Anton requested, starts to look around for clues. For slips of paper or writings or anything that might offer some suggestion as to whether Ben had a plan or just up and left. She finds only the usual scraps— lists of places or things to accomplish: *New fence posts with Carolyn*, one note reads. *Tell Renny thank you*, another note says. *Call Jess and ask how she is*. It's all the mishmash of a brain trying to right itself, like a boat at sea seeking balance.

Between the dark hours of midnight and daybreak, while the blizzard is in full force and the sky is socked in with black thick fury, she calls Carolyn's cell phone. She tells herself that she's calling for one reason, which is that Carolyn will not forgive her if Ben is found dead and frozen and Renny had not called. But really, she only wants to hear another human voice. There is no one, though. Only a clicking noise. Perhaps there is no service.

She walks to Ben's drawer and rifles through it again. Then she goes through his laundry, pulling scraps from his jeans. Now she's angry. She's tired and wants to go to sleep. Where *is* he?

She searches in earnest now, throwing clothes and items all over the place. Satchmo runs around her, excited, picking up shoes and dropping them. In one corner of the closet, she finds more lists.

Feed chickens (7 chickens)
Feed donkeys (4)
Feed horses (2)
Check cabin
Call Eddie
Ruben

Or:
Check on Jess. Watershed of the heart
Goodbye = back away = water runs backward

Or:
I am married to Renny. I am Ben Cross. Born May 5, 1934, Greeley Colorado. Hell's Bottom Ranch. Two daughters.

Or:
I am a dummy.

That last one slows her down, but she tosses it to the side and keeps up her search. She finds pocketknives and the glasses he has been missing for weeks. She finds money, stashed away in the toes of his cowboy boots. She finds river stones that must hold some meaning. She is disgusted that everything is so dusty and that she let it get that way. She finds the bleached white of a raccoon skull. She finds an envelope labeled *Instructions to Ben Cross*, but when she opens it, there is nothing in there.

She walks through the house and then sits at her desk, littered with her calendar and various farm bills and receipts and bookkeeping, the bill of sale from the cattle they sold a year ago, and which she needs for this year's taxes, paper clips and tape and an old letter from Jess.

When Anton calls to report that they haven't seen him and to ask if she has any news, she tells him she's found nothing. He ends the call by saying, "Renny, do you think it had anything to do with today, at the cemetery? I saw you two, and then I saw him yelling. What set him off? Did he want to go somewhere?" and Renny's brain feels like a snowstorm, she can't think, but all she says is, "No, no, I don't think so, it's just that you look like Ray, is all, we've both noted that before, and maybe this time, when he saw you across . . . well, I think he mistook you," and Anton says, "Renny, this storm. It's ten below right now," and Renny says, "I know it, I've been watching the news," and then there is a pause before he hangs up, a pause that means *Renny, prepare.*

Renny closes her eyes and thinks of the cemetery, of the yelling. Ben was angry, more angry than she's ever seen him. At Ray. Ray. Ray.

And then she knows. She picks up the phone, pauses, puts it back down. Son of a bitch. She stands, walks to her bedroom quickly, dresses in warm thick fleece pants and hiking boots and a sweater. She packs a small bag quickly, she calculates things in her mind: buses have many stops, her truck has four-wheel drive, Ben knew Ray was in Greeley and could remember that because it was also the town of his birth, and she wouldn't mind seeing Ray herself. She and Ben will face him, one last time, together.

BEN

The restaurant's lights have been dimmed so that people can sleep. It appears that most are, heads on hands, although a few have stretched out on the gray tile floor. The waitress, the one with the belly growing in her stomach, has sat down next to Ben and fallen asleep leaning against him. She breathes like a small windmill. He can hear the cook still making something and a few people murmur over in one corner, but it is mostly quiet.

Ben wishes he could sleep but instead watches the woman's belly, which is round like the moon and rises and falls just like the moon. Across from him, the boy-man has fallen asleep, leaning back against the wall, his legs out across the seat of the booth, and Ben recognizes the horse on his shirt, which is the Bronco from the football team. The boy snores about every third breath and moves his jaw and scratches his arms in his sleep and sometimes says a whole bunch of words mashed up together or sometimes simply says one word, which is always *fuck*.

Ben can't remember why he's here. *That's okay*, he tells himself. *Hold steady. It will come to you.* Besides, he knows Renny will come help him. She'll be here soon. He misses holding Renny and he misses sex, a word that comes to him suddenly with the shock of memory of what it was like, and for a moment, he is happy. Then suddenly some dust blows and he remembers Ray. *Go away, Ray, get out of my brain, Ray, bring my daughter back, Ray, you are in Greeley, Ray.* And then he thinks a calmer thought which is *I miss you, Rachel. I hope I get to see you, Rachel. In the next life, Rachel. Are you there?* And then his brain circulates like a dryer that is going round and round:

> *Go away, Ray.*
> *I miss you, Rachel.*
> *Hell's Bottom.*
> *Go away, out of my brain, Ray.*
> *What are my granddaughters' names?*
> *Leanne. Jess.*
> *Yes, Leanne. Jess.*
> *Renny.*
> *Where's Renny?*
> *I miss Renny.*

Are there other grandkids? He can't remember. But he does remember the games Renny used to play with him to keep his mind active: list your grandkids, list all the dogs we've ever had, list the places you've been.

He bit off the tip of his tongue. That's what it feels like. He can't remember the words that live on the tip of his tongue.

Then he is crying, and the crying wakes the waitress, who sits up and says, "Oh, honey, it's going to be okay."

He wants to say that his brain feels worse than ever, that he is terrified that he soon won't realize it, that this is the last thing he will ever know about his brain.

"The storm will end soon. I bet they have the roads cleared by morning. You can get back on the bus. Where you heading, anyway?"

He shrugs and wipes at his eyes with his sleeve.

She regards him. "You should get some sleep, hon. It's going to be okay."

"My brain's not so good," he says now, and he realizes, with a pang of clarity, that this waitress chose to sleep next to him because he needed her, he was the most fragile, she was worried that someone would rob or hurt him, that she was taking care of him the way a rancher would take care of an injured animal. Her pregnancy makes her this way. He's so grateful. What a kindness. "My brain . . . But I'm not as dummy as people think I am."

"Aw, now, mister, you don't look like a dummy at all."

"I just can't find the right words. I know I can't find the right words. But that doesn't mean I'm not thinking them. That I don't know what I want to say. I do know. I do have things to say."

"Well, that must be awfully hard then."

"But there's no use complaining." He hears the sorrow in his own voice.

"Well. But sometimes it helps." The woman sits up and stretches and rubs her belly. "Oh lordy, my feet hurt. See? It helps a little to say that. To share it with someone. And there's always hope."

"No!" He says it suddenly, surprising them both. "There's not." After the doctor said, *Dementia, probably Alzheimer's given your age*, that's when he'd understood again that hope is a bad emotion. Because then you're hoping about the future

113

and not paying attention to now. Because hope is sometimes just a joke. He touches the moon-woman's arm. "Tell ya what I'm gonna do, see. I'm not going to hope. Now, you don't either. Don't hope your life will get better. Just make it so. Don't hope you are able to handle this baby. Just do it. Just be glad, just move fast, just do what you need to do. But for god's sake, don't hope. Just be . . . Just *be* . . ."

She looks at him sadly and says, "Sure, sure."

"Rachel. I had a daughter named Rachel."

"Oh?"

"And her husband. Whose name is Ray."

"Okay."

"Ray, who killed her."

"Oh, my god. I'm so sorry. That's . . . horrible." She leans into him. "We forget how some people are horrible, don't we? Your own child. Oh god. We just assume . . ." and then puts her arm around him.

"He was in Cañon City."

"Yes, the prison."

"They released him now. His time is up, they say. But it hasn't been very long. And I don't think he's a better man."

"Oh," she says. "I'm so sorry. That makes it far worse, huh?"

"I'm going to visit him." He sees that startles her. "Because I need to see him. Because I gave my family bad genetics. Bad DNA. That protein. That lysosome," and now he is crying, tears sliding down his cheeks like a quiet rain, and the words come out more freely because of the tears. "But he did it on purpose."

The belly-woman reaches out to hold his hand. He realizes he has hurt her, that she is crying, and he nods when she says she better attend to some things but that she'll come back with something for him to eat. He remembers Renny yelling at him

114

about watching football and how it was a waste of time, of precious time. Why couldn't he ever talk about something real? Renny was right about everything.

He puts his jacket under his head and stretches out, his legs along the booth, although the booth is not long enough. Across the room is a young woman, a girl even, who had been on the bus. The one who looks like his dead daughter. She's in a booth, sleeping with her head turned away, and the wool shirt she wears is just like one he used to have, gray plaid with a bit of red. Probably she is alone and scared too.

He doesn't want to be a burden. To the waitress, bus driver, Renny. He told Renny to move him to assisted living a long time ago, so that he could get used to it, but she'd said, *They'll just let you rot. They won't make you* do *things, and doing things is how your brain is going to last.* He can hear her voice exactly. Her love was tough, but it was real.

But he didn't even mean it, wanting to move to assisted living. He was just feeling his options out. He wants to die on the ranch. *Remember*, he says over and over, *you want to die on the ranch. Or at least outside.*

He let Renny take him, once, to a living place. Last week or maybe yesterday. Jess went too. Jess drove them both into town and they went on a tour. It was a big place and was just how he imagined it would be, clean and friendly with a big room in the middle with a TV and a chess table and other tables and a room for eating and a bedroom that was small and tidy and had a view of a parking lot.

When he stood inside, looking out at the parking lot, that's when he knew he would take his life. But he didn't want to use the gun, too messy, too loud, and too much like Ray and Rachel. And Jess had touched his arm and said, "Grandpa Ben? This place isn't for you."

He wanted something quieter to do his quiet life justice. It was the first time he thought about how he wanted to die, and he realized he wanted to die facing the sky. He wrote a letter about it, didn't he?

"That was an important moment, not like the Broncos," he says now, but no one hears him and no one stirs. Perhaps he falls asleep, and in his half dreams he recalls the mountain lions and the black bear and the foxes. He dreams of the things he killed and the things he did not. He dreams of animals. In his dreams, he tells himself he should dream of people, concentrate on people, but he keeps dreaming of animals instead, and they are so wild and beautiful and he knows that deep down they are one and the same.

RENNY

Renny has engaged the four-wheel drive. Although she goes slowly, she goes in the sure knowledge that the highway patrol has closed the roads but that, as always, she is exempt from all dumb rules. Besides, the deputies have better things to do than to stop her, and also, she's lived in Colorado all her life and not once has she misjudged a slippery blizzard road, which is saying something given the number of snowstorms she has seen come and go, the number of blizzards she braved in order to haul newborn calves into the kitchen, or in order to feed animals, or find them, or round them up for shelter. This is not that bad; the media and police are always exaggerating everything. *Everyone* exaggerates everything, she thinks now, because it makes them feel important. The stupid human need to feel important. Plus, she's avoiding the highway and taking the back roads to Greeley, and she's been to Greeley plenty of times—she and Ben used to drive there regularly to visit his folks, back when they were still alive, and to visit their gravestones once they were dead. He'd recently been pestering her to take him to Greeley, pester pester, and it made her crazy. "Drive yourself," she would say, although she knew it was cruel, that he couldn't, and that he'd probably give about anything to accomplish a simple task like that again.

She can see the faint lights of Ault. AULT: A UNIQUE LITTLE TOWN, their sign says, and it's really the only town on the way to Greeley. Once she makes it to Ault, she'll be on Highway 85, which will no doubt be plowed, and which always makes her feel safe since the highway is split by a track of grasslands and she's always appreciated the lack of things coming right *at* her. She'll pass the sugar beet factory and the sheep farms and the silos. As long as the windshield wipers are going full speed and the headlights make the reflectors on the intermittent green posts shine, and she drives carefully, she'll get there. The road has been plowed once, and although it's getting covered up again quickly, she can make out the slight distinction between plowed and unplowed by the way the headlights catch the shadow of the difference. She's got four-wheel drive. The road is flat and deserted. There's nothing to run in *to*. Just go carefully forward. She'll make it.

She'll get there and find her husband at the Greyhound bus station. She'll see Ray, although she's not sure how, although she remembers the County Road EE. She will be guided to the one or both of them by instinct. She will face, with her husband, the man who murdered their daughter.

Satchmo sits next to her, panting and sometimes whining. She should have brought her some food, but she forgot that, along with probably ten million other things. She reaches under the seat where Ben keeps a bag of beef jerky and hands Satchmo a big piece. She turns on the radio to discover that radio waves are not stopped by storms at all, and a bit of jazz comes floating through the cab of the truck. Satchmo lays down then, head on Renny's lap, makes a small whine, and thumps her tail.

"You might not be so bad after all," she tells the dog.

Up ahead, she sees the bright and erratic lights of what must be a snowplow, though she can't see the vehicle itself at all. It's coming toward her, lights like a UFO surrounded in a wall of white, and she puts on her blinker and starts to pull as far as she can to the edge of the road. Then the whish of the air, of the snow, of the machine itself. Satchmo lets out a bark as Renny jerks on the steering wheel, realizing she is still too close, she is going to be hit. Her truck is smacked by an enormous amount of snow—an incredible thud—and then, as if it were the most natural and right thing to do, her truck simply heads down the small irrigation ditch. She feels it start to tip, pause, almost right itself. She holds her breath, clutches the seat belt, reaches out to hold the dog against the seat. The truck tilts, slowly, thirty degrees, forty-five degrees, sixty degrees—it seems impossible, it's such a small incline!—but like a math problem she needs to help a grandchild with, like some imaginary problem come real, it is enough of an incline.

Impossible.

She braces before the noise of her truck hitting snow. It's a loud thud, but no crashing, no splintering. So loud, and then so calm. She feels vomit in her throat as she slides sideways into the seat belt and also into the dog and the dog is barking, climbing over her, and her shoulder hurts and the dog's claws tear through her sweater, and then, suddenly, there is pure and real silence.

The truck, on its side, stalls out. The dog is still clawing past her leg and she turns, hoping to see the snowplow stop—thinking that he must stop—but blinking lights are receding in the distance. She reaches out with her left hand and presses on the horn and the noise seems loud enough to stop anything but the snowplow has disappeared.

Impossible.

It creeps in on her: He never saw her. She and Satchmo are miles from anyone, in the middle of the night and in the middle of a blizzard, and no one knows where they are.

"Okay, let me think here. I can't believe that just . . . happened. Satchmo, shut the hell up." She unbuckles and lets herself slide to the window of the pickup and crouches there and feels around in the dark for her purse. She feels it with her hand, the smooth feel of leather, and she clutches it to her. She leans up and turns the ignition off, then halfway on, so that the headlights are again beaming into the night. Only then can she see the wind whip and rise and tear around. One light is high up, one is at ground level, and their beams intersect in the far distance.

From the glove compartment, she finds the cool cylinder of the flashlight. As she turns it on, the dog whines. She casts the light about the cab. She can see her own arm, the dog, the Valentine card Ben made her, the junk from the dash, all of it scattered around her on the passenger-side door and window. The dog has a cut on her forehead and is bleeding and Renny reaches out to feel it and can tell, with her fingers, that it is not deep or large, and that the dog is fine. Still, she says, "Oh, Satchmo. Sorry about that. Don't worry."

Oh, god. She can't breathe. What is she supposed to do? The wind outside is howling so loud that she can't think. Or perhaps it is Satchmo that is whining. Perhaps it is the universe?

Did she bump her head? Or is this seasick dizziness just nerves? She must be smart here. She must think. She must get her brain to work. She considers: If there was one snowplow, there will be another. If Anton goes to her house, he will find her missing. If she can start the truck, she can stay warm. On the other hand, she needs to make sure the exhaust isn't covered; she doesn't want to die of carbon monoxide. And the truck has, in fact, fallen on the side with the exhaust. She has the cell phone in her purse, doesn't she? She must think, she must think. But over all this, twining through all this, is a simple childlike surprise. She never would have thought this. It simply seems impossible. She expected Ben to die, and that she would live. She's thought plenty about Ben's death; she's been saying good-bye in various ways for some time now. But she hasn't even begun the process—*and how could this be?*—of saying good-bye to herself.

Vomit rises and she chokes as she swallows it down. Everything depends on the cell phone, and she's forever forgetting to charge it, just like she forever forgets things like bringing mint for tea. With the purse tucked under her chin, and a flashlight in one hand, she tugs open the zipper and feels inside until her hand wraps around her phone. She turns it on, and miraculously, it lights up. 9-1-1. Only one other time has she called this number. Seventy-two years on this planet and she's dialed it once, in order to save her daughter, and it was too late. By the time she heard the sirens, her daughter was in her arms, bleeding from her head all over. Convulsing. Shaking. Convulsing. Dead. By the time she heard the sirens, Ray had raced out, Ben had raced out after him, shouting after the black Ford truck that was peeling out of the driveway and then falling to his knees. By the time they came, her daughter's eyes had turned still and although she had slapped her and screamed and tore off her own shirt to staunch the blood the eyes were still.

Only once she has asked for help. It didn't come. And so that part of her died. The part that is willing to reach out and ask. Be tender in that way. Because, for god's sake, if you go through life and hardly ask for anything—and then you ask once, just once!—and there's no response, well, then, the hell with it.

9-1-1. She punches it in, praying to all the good people who know how to help. "Please," she says aloud, "please-oh-god-please."

The wind howls and whistles around her as she waits, listening, for something on the other end. She holds her breath, waiting. It would be nice if, for once, she could count deeply on someone else.

BEN

The restaurant is so bright and loud against the dark of night and storm. People are waking and food is served and a baby cries and the boy-man paces and moves his jaw and scratches his wrists and cusses and the girl in the gray-plaid shirt reads a book. Ben gets up to stretch his legs and use the bathroom and a few folks stand for a moment or two outside the door so as to see the storm and feel the cold tight air that sucks at their lungs. He looks at a book that has been handed to him, but he can't read small words anymore, only the big words on signs. He has no other way to pass the time and wishes for a football game but instead he watches people, cranky and hopeful, and one woman is crying in the corner. He closes his eyes and thinks of red willows and dark-eyed horses and how both ripple with the joy of the world.

There are people with phones. He knows he should call but he cannot remember the number. He knows his wife's name is Renny but he can't remember the second name that comes after the first. He looks up to find the girl staring at him. It makes him feel shame, so he looks at a chain that's hanging from his wrist. Why is it there? Has he been in jail?

Water fills his eyes and spills over and he wonders about the source of that water, how at one time it was in the sea.

"Aw, mister. You want me to call someone?" The waitress is rubbing her moon and he shakes his head, no, and then, to make sure she doesn't worry, he goes into the bathroom to comb his hair and swish water to get rid of the thick taste in his mouth.

Finally the bus driver stands up and yells something. The sun will soon be up, the man says, and the plows have gone through and although it's still snowing, they will continue on.

Ben follows the others into the whipping snow underneath a black sky. He boards the bus and finds a seat and he is glad, so glad, that the boy-man sits elsewhere and that he is left alone. Ben has his jacket, his wallet, and his suitcase. He knows he's done a good job. He is worried that someone is going to stop him, but in fact no one does.

The bus pulls out of the big parking lot slowly, bumping over a poorly snowplowed area, and then onto the highway. A few people cheer, but Ben can tell that it's going to be slowgoing, very slow. From the side window he can see only the flakes hitting and melting or the ones whizzing close by. It seems to him that the snow is very tender. Or trying to be.

Sometimes they pass signs or small towns and one lit-up sign advertises FILM * GIFTS * OXYGEN and another THE FAMOUS GROUSE. He passes a trailer house that also has a lit sign in the darkness, and it says it is a library and it makes him sad, such a small space for so many huge ideas. The snowplows pass every once in a while, throwing white on the windows, and he likes to watch their power, likes to know that they are clearing the roads so that he can go back to Renny. There are two pieces of paper in his pocket, and he gets both out to hold in his hands.

It is not so long—hardly time to nap, even, although he feels himself fall asleep for a while—when the bus driver stops the bus and says, "Greeley," and when Ben doesn't move, the bus driver comes back. "Greeley, sir. Your stop," and Ben hands him the note.

The man looks at one and squints and hands it back and says, "Don't know what this one means," and Ben looks down to see numbers and letters, something about ccs, and some other words that he doesn't quite remember although he feels embarrassed that the man has seen it. The other note the man reads aloud. "My name is Ben Cross. I'm trying to get to Greeley, Colorado," and he says, "Well, Gramps, you made it, this here is Greeley." So Ben does what the man wants, which is to grab his suitcase and get off in the dark night with the snow slapping his face in small little bits of pain. The blizzard is not so bad here as it was near the mountains, and the snow only goes up past his ankles, wetting his socks.

The bus station is really just a car lot with a small lit building, and he ducks his head and walks inside. Some others get off with him, then they seem to disappear, into waiting cars or out into the dark. Only a few mill about, the boy with the *bok-bok* face and that girl too, but they disappear in the back of the room, where he can't see.

He needs to think. What was he going to do now? He just needs to rest, to get some peace and quiet. His brain is tired from being with those people in that restaurant and eating all that pie. Soon he will know what to do.

He carries his suitcase with him into the men's room, which he knows is the men's because he has double-checked for the stick drawing of a man. In the bathroom he tries to pee but cannot. He tries for a long time to open the suitcase but he cannot figure out the latch. Finally the suitcase falls open and inside is a clean button-down shirt and he puts it on. There is also a toothbrush and so he brushes his teeth, because they feel very dirty. He washes his face in the sink and dries it with brown paper towels. There is nothing else in the suitcase and so he stares at it for a long time, wondering why he's been lugging this suitcase around with only a shirt and toothbrush. Wasn't there something else in here? Wasn't he going to use it if worse came to worse?

He sits on the toilet and finally a small stream comes and he tries to think of Ray's last name. Ray who was with Rachel. Rachel Cross. And then, he feels himself leaning, falling asleep, right there on the toilet, propping himself up with his arms, which are braced on his knees. Later, in his sleep, he feels himself move to the floor of the bathroom, where he continues sleeping, and then he dreams that someone is above him, moving his face onto a shirt.

When he wakes, his face is indeed pressed against a shirt that he does not recognize. And he feels that someone he knows put it there—was it his daughter? The one who died? And then it comes to him, like a gift. That is why he is here: Ray Steele.

He climbs up, pees, washes himself, and then walks out. Yes, Ray Steele.

He can't remember exactly where he is, but he's in a small room, but he senses that, like nature, it will unfold correctly. There's a short-haired older woman sitting behind a desk, and the woman says, "Oh!" when he walks toward her. And then she says, "Where did you come from? I didn't know anyone else was here! Were you on that delayed bus?" and she glances at the two or three others, sitting in the yellow chairs, and then she peers at him, and says, "What can I help you with, sir? Need a ticket somewhere?"

He nods at her, trying to form words. "See, I'll tell you what. See." He reaches into his pocket and hands her some slips of paper and she reads them and looks at him, then glances at the papers and then at him again.

And then she says, "Why, you are Ben Cross. Oh, I love when small towns are still small towns."

"Ben Cross, yes. That's me."

"Well, I'll be. Criminy. I suppose you don't remember me. There's no reason you should. You went to high school with my older sister. She's a teacher now. Or was. She's been retired for some time. I was four grades younger, though. But I remember you. Watching you play baseball."

"Oh, that," he says. "Those were some good days."

"Oh, they sure were. I was at your parents' funerals. Probably you don't remember. You own a ranch up north, right?"

"Hell's Bottom Ranch," he says, so happy that his tongue found the words. "Prettiest place on earth."

"Oh, I believe it," she says. "I do. My name is Rachelle Forkner, by the way. Maybe you remember me? My folks owned the grocery."

"Oh, sure," Ben says, and he has a memory of walking in there when he was young, a list of items written in his mother's perfect Palmer handwriting, and checking them off. Eggs, butter, vanilla, that white stuff that makes bread. "My mind isn't what it used to be, but I remember things back that far, sure."

"Some storm out there. Horrible. Glad the electricity is on, though. Glad the bus made it. They might be shutting down I-25 again, I hear. It's worse up near you. Where you left from, I mean. And of course, all the side roads are down."

"A bad one, yes."

"Well, it sure is good to see you." She hands back the slips of paper.

He hesitates, wondering if he should trust her. "I'm here looking for a man. Ray Steele."

She scratches her head with the tip of a ball point pen. "Ray Steele. Never heard of him. Greeley's gotten pretty big, you know. Gangs and all that. Meth and so on. The downtown part is nice, though. And the campus is still nice."

Ben looks at his shoes. Then he remembers the bigger piece of paper in his suitcase and pulls it out. It's an old creased newspaper account of the murder, and he slides it across the counter to her. She reads it, shaking her head and making clucking noises like a chicken, which makes him wonder about his chickens and makes him worry about Renny.

"I remember reading this. Didn't remember the name of the man, though. This town has gotten so big I don't recognize people anymore. He's in Greeley now, you say? He probably rode the bus, got off right before my eyes, and I wouldn't have known him. A murderer! He probably took a bus from the prison to here. Great. I miss Greeley the way it used to be. The way that Mr. Horace Greeley intended it. And here we got a murderer in our vicinity." Then she stops, peers at him closer. "You came to see him? Your family know where you are?"

Ben opens his mouth and closes it. If he could just ask for what he wants, if he could just remember what to say. Instead he says, "Well, sure. We have an . . . appointment. Boy, my mind's not working so good. That bus trip and sleeping in the café. That was a bit hard on my old brain."

The woman peers at him a moment and then says, "Hang on a minute, Ben," and he sees that she's making a phone call, and then another. He shifts his weight—just like an old horse, he thinks—and glances around the room. There's a girl that is wearing a flannel shirt, just like one he used to have, and she's got her head buried in her hands, sleeping.

He wants Renny here. But there's something he alone needs to do. And the woman is still on the phone. Finally, out of sheer weariness, he leaves the counter and sits in one of the yellow chairs, next to the girl. Finally, the phone-woman waves him over. "All right, Ben. I called around and got hold of Ray Steele. The criminal element in this community is all connected, although that's very unchristian of me, perhaps they're all turning their lives around, including Ray. Ray, I spoke to that man myself." Here, she widens her eyes, looking startled at herself for being startled in the first place. "I don't get surprised by much these days. Can't believe I had it in me. But he said he wrote you a letter, asking for a visit. So I guess it's all right. He says he's coming here, to this building, as soon as he digs his truck out, and it shouldn't be much longer. He lives a little out of town, though, on a county road." She pauses and cocks her head. "You came here to see him? I think that's mighty brave, Ben Cross."

Ben nods and some of the dust clears and he can hear his words and that his words come out in the right order. "He killed my daughter. He got let out of prison. I figured while there was still time I ought to look him in the eye."

"Well, I'll be. No joke. That's something, Ben." Then she pauses, clears her throat. "I hope you don't mind, Ben, but I also called your home. Found your number in information. I just left a message on your machine. I suppose your wife would want to know that you were here and all, after the blizzard. Or at least I would, if I were married to you. Did you call her?"

He pats his pockets and says, "I lost my . . ."

"Cell phone?"

"Well, that thing in my suitcase—"

"Well, dang. That's no good. But that's why I called her. Just to let her know. I can redial the number, if you want to leave a message yourself."

"Oh, that's okay. Thank you kindly."

"She knows you're here?"

"Oh sure."

"Well. I don't know why she let you out of the house in such a storm. I remember her being a bit . . . ornery. Anyway. Here, have some coffee. Sun's about to come up." She hands him a white cup and a white powdery donut from a bag that she's got behind the counter.

"Oh sure." He takes a sip and thinks of the last time he saw Renny, holding her at the cemetery, saying that he was going inside to take a nap, and she knew, she knew, she knew that was not his plan. She knew the plan, he's sure of it. "If you don't mind," he says, and then indicates the restroom with a tilt of his head.

Ray Steele is coming. This man was . . . What was he to do? . . . His brain can't think it through, but his heart seems to know, because it's revving up to the point he is going to be sick. Maybe his heart will take it from here? The brain has checked out but the body still doing good. *Revving of heart = courage* is all he can think, and he knows it doesn't make sense.

He stands at the window trying to calm the rev and keep his stomach from coming out his mouth. It hurts his brain to focus on the signs so therefore it feels important. In the gusting white world lit by streetlamps he sees GREELEY MONUMENT WORKS. FRANK'S SEED AND HATCHERY. LOT CLOSED FOR FARMERS' MARKET WEDNESDAY AND SATURDAY. He looks at the hedges and blooms of pure white snow, watches a snowplow go *beep-beeping* by in the dark. He looks at the old depot, at the metal silos, and now he knows where he is—close to the road that will take him to the farm where he was born, to the place where he became a man.

It's right that he's here.

He goes back into the bathroom and sits, relieves himself, and sits some more. Gets his heart and vomit to go back down where they should be. He remembers when the doctor said, *Dementia, probably Alzheimer's*, and he remembers the snap of heartbreak and fear. He wishes he could go just a few minutes without feeling his disease. Just a few moments of clarity.

He pulls out a slip of paper from his pocket. *My name is Ben Cross. I am trying to get to Greeley, Colorado.* It takes him a long time to understand why he wrote that, but then he pats the pocket of his jacket and pulls out a small bottle of liquid and two syringes wrapped in plastic.

There was something important, but his mind can't catch it. He decides now just to trust the instinct.

He unwraps the plastic—he has to use his teeth—and takes off the cap from the syringe. Sticks it in the bottle. The liquid is very thick and thus his needle is a large bore, 18-gauge, and requires a bit of strength and patience. He's glad he's still strong. He's glad he's operating out of habit. Because of habit and know-how, he can pull the liquid back into the syringe, all the way to the top, 20 ccs. He remembers that a one-thousand-pound horse would get 100 ccs, and so a two-hundred-pound man would get 20, he knows this by instinct and not by thought, and he's aware of the difference.

Trust your heart and gut, he hears himself saying, *not your brain. Probably you already did anyway.* He doesn't know what he means by that, even, but the words repeat themselves over and over. Aloud or inside his head, he doesn't know. It doesn't matter anymore. He is in a world that doesn't quite operate in the usual way.

He knows how to do this from pure repetition. He has done it so many times before. To keep animals from suffering. Always, to stave away suffering. He fills up two. It takes a long time but his hands are steady. He realizes, as he finishes, that he had brought a gun as backup, and now the gun is gone, and that it has been stolen or lost, and that now he has only this, and he must do it right.

He remembers Esme saying, *The moments of joy, when you connect with the Alzheimer's patient, will get less frequent.* It sounds like a poem. Then he remembers a memory. Of him telling himself something. Telling himself something important. Courage and fear and prayers. He remembers seeing Renny's journal. THE SAD STORY OF RENNY AND BEN. He wonders what she was writing when she hunched over it and scratched something.

Something is hurting his foot. He puts the syringes in his pocket and sits on the toilet seat, pants still on. He takes off his shoe and—huh!—there is a piece of paper stuck to the bottom of his sock. *Well, I'll be. How'd that get there?* INSTRUCTIONS FOR BEN CROSS, it says on the outside. It takes him a moment to figure out the words, but he can do it. It's in his own handwriting and indeed he can even catch the fleeting memory of writing it, his own hand scratching out the marks in pencil. He cannot read well and holds it far from his eyes. Now he can see the words but they do not connect with a meaning in his mind. He shuts his eyes and says to his brain, *please*, and breathes in and out, quietly. But no. It's not coming. He closes his eyes and begs. Begs.

Then there is a girl in the bathroom, and now he knows he is dying or that his brain is really gone. She is a dream or an angel. He didn't get to do his job in time. He stays seated on the toilet, puts his head in his hands, and tries to ready himself for a good-bye to the soul of Ben Cross.

But when he opens his eyes, she is still there, holding the paper, reading in a whisper. At first he doesn't understand and she reads it over and over like a song stuck on repeat, and finally he lets the confusion of it all go away and he closes his eyes and listens. As he does, he has a flicker of a memory. Writing this. What it means. He feels his heart tinker or flicker or something like glitter.

Instructions to Ben Cross:

Dear Ben,

You are a rancher in Colorado.

You had two daughters and you've lived a good life.

You have been a good man.

You have Alzheimer's.

I just found that out about me. Heart broke. But I stayed strong and steady. Tell you what I'm gonna do, see.

I'm keeping this simple for you.

You don't want to be like that horse that ran around, suffering. You deserve to go quick. Believe me. Trust me. I've been you my entire life, so trust me now. Do the following:

1. Pink juice
2. Fill syringe.

3. Directly into the heart. It will take two hands, lot of force. Think of the horses. You've done this many times with the big animals. So you can do it. Punch hard. This is the right thing to do. The main thing I have to tell you is: Do it. Don't back out. Don't forget. Do this thing.

Good luck, Ben. Be brave.

It's been a good life.

Willows, orange in the winter and green in the summer.

Aspen trees.

Mountains.

Everyone has to die, Ben. No life without death. And your time is now, and it's okay. Do it fast. Trust me.

RENNY

For once, something has gone her way. The 9-1-1 call goes through. She hears the operator, she hears her own voice yelp, "In car, blizzard, please, Ault, truck tipped," and she hears, "Your name?" then the phone beeps, goes dead. She holds the phone as she stares out into the dark night, the snow lit up by one headlight.

Perhaps it is enough? Anton has told her stories before, of how they triangulate 9-1-1 calls, something she was impressed by even as she judged the poor moron who got himself in the situation that required it in the first place.

"For god's sake," she says aloud, meaning to get the attention of universe. "When is enough going to be enough?"

She finds that she's sitting on the door and glass of the passenger side of the truck, leaning back against the edge of the seat, Satchmo clawing at her, whining and shaking. Her own butt is frozen—the cold seeps right in through the window—and she's starting to shake. From fear or cold, she doesn't know. She hopes fear. Fear doesn't kill you.

She fingers the dog's ears and jowls and whispers *good dog good dog* over and over. The sky is black except for the beams of the truck's headlights, which is how she can see the snow rushing at her. The engine is off and the truck is cooling quickly. Amazing, how cold it's become already. Amazing, how fast nature takes over.

The flashlight flicks off and the inside of the cab is surprisingly dark. She whacks the flashlight twice on the dashboard to make it work and then, in the light, twists this way and that way, grunting, heaving the dog momentarily to the side so she can reach the blanket under the seat. The blanket is from Mexico and has a beautiful bright pattern but is only minimally warm. She shoves it under her butt and folds the corners over her and Satchmo. Then she grabs the first aid kit that usually rests underneath the seat but has come to rest on the dash. Inside she finds a space blanket and she unwraps and unfolds the thin shiny material, but it seems ridiculous, unable to do the task for which it was designed. There's nothing else useful in the kit, really, but she likes knowing it's there.

From where she is huddled on the truck door and window, she stares at the keys dangling in the ignition. She should start the truck, but only if the exhaust isn't blocked. And what about leaking fluids and gas? What if she explodes?

No, she doesn't want to die by falling asleep and she doesn't want to explode. She'd rather see it coming.

So this is it.

As her shivers become solid and constant, she feels the knowledge seep in. She doesn't know how to prepare for it, to prepare for the darkness, to prepare for God or not-God. She wonders if the afterlife is made up of what you believe, which makes her think that she doesn't even have a clear vision of what she hopes for. She remembers how Esme once brought in a Buddhist to teach meditation to the Alzheimer's group, and she tries that now. *Breathing in, peace. Breathing out, peace.*

Also, that woman said to write a letter, she remembers now. A good-bye letter to life. She digs around the dash for a pen and grabs Ben's Valentine's Day card. *Febuary 16/17*, she writes on the soft pink paper on the back. She holds the flashlight in the crook of her neck and writes as fast as she can.

Dear Life, Dear Everyone:

It's a little hard to write a good-bye letter to you, because I don't want to go. That's the truth of it. I want someone to acknowledge that this dying business is as bad as Lipton tea. Bitter and empty and nothing beautiful. No flavor, no spice. No one wants it. At least without a little lemon and sugar, as in, something beautiful to hold on to. But none is provided. Thanks a lot, Universe.

But you, those whom I love, you were spice and flavor. I thank you for that. So was the ranch. I hope you know that. If not, I'm telling you now.

I know that there is no life without death. So here goes.

I think I tried pretty hard. I think I tried to rise to the occasion of life. Maybe I failed, but it often seemed as if I was tired from trying.

I think it's a little unfair and unkind that all of humanity has been left so alone in this regard. That we have no solace, no answers. I think it's hard that we're so alone in this. I feel very alone. I don't say that to make you feel bad. You'll be alone too someday. It's the nature of this.

She thinks she probably ought to wrap it up, but, on the other hand, she's got to occupy herself with something. There's nothing to be done. There's nothing she can do. She's trapped and claustrophobic in a small truck in a huge blizzard. She closes her eyes and lets the tears force themselves out of the eyelids. Writing will keep the panic at bay. So she keeps going.

Ray was horrible. What he did to us was horrible. But I love all the rest of you. Carolyn and Jess and Billy and Leanne and Jack and Ben and the friends and neighbors we have. I'm sorry for any meanness I ever threw at you, I hope you'll remember anything nice I ever did. I'll miss you. If dead people can miss. I'll miss the clouds when they boil up over the mountains. I'll miss Jess on her horse. I'll miss watching the birds nest in spring and watching the mama and dad bird bring them food, one after the other.

I tried. Love to you all. Renny.

And by now, her hand is shaking and the last words are hardly legible. Her whole body is shaking, and about every half minute, the shakes turn into a convulsion. *Here goes*, she thinks. Here goes. She puts down the flashlight and tries to breathe in peace, but all she can feel is the fear, a disgusting roar of cowardly fear that sounds as loud as the wind. They're both howling and whistling like a creature that is alive, like a devil, like something ready to kill her. She is shaking and cannot stop. Howling like all meanness, like the hurt of a daughter in the ground, like the wasted life of living on a ranch with a man who didn't love her, who got sick and needed her anyway. Howling and howling.

This dying business, she writes in the margin. *It's not what I thought it would be. Sorry about Satchmo. We're both shaking. I thought it would be a little more settled and kind than this.*

She holds Satchmo to her, tight. Looks out at the dark night. She's seen it happen to calves and to colts. The shaking as the body cools and tries to warm itself. Ben did love her. Ben loved her despite her hardness. He saw her spirit, saw something to appreciate about it. What would she do if she lived? She wants to complain about her grandchildren's behavior. She wants to see her family on holidays and she even wants them to mess up her house. She hadn't thought it through before, but she thinks it through now. She wants to die in the company of friends and family whom she has been kind to. She wants Ben there, the old Ben. God, how she loved how he quietly looked at the world. How he would smile and see all the way through her yapping.

Where did she get the ridiculous notion that people lived a full life and then died in peace? She didn't know she was going to die with a broken heart. Die with so much hurt. Why did she think it was the other way around? Whatever gave her that stupid idea?

She leans over and vomits behind the seat, trying to avoid the dog, and then she places her hands on her heaving stomach muscles to calm them.

She is so cold. And so this is it? Yes, this is it. She will die of exposure.

The knowledge comes at her like a big dust cloud, just like in the photos of the dust bowl of her infancy, a big billowy dark cloud. Just like Ben's brain, she knows now. She can see it coming. Death. Death is the dust cloud, boiling and roiling over the wind-seared plains outside her window. She can't see out there. She can't see anything, because the snow has picked up and the headlights are covered and buried now. The dog whines. She is shivering huge shivers that aren't even shivers as much as they are spasms.

She turns off the flashlight and leans her head back. She doesn't need it now so much anyway. The daylight is slowly working its way into being.

She should move. She should force herself to do one last thing. She should dig out her headlights. She pauses to consider the logistics of this, to think through the steps. She realizes that this is what Ben has to do about everything—think through the steps. By god, if he's been doing that for who knows how long, she can do this one thing. The only problem is she can't tell if it's a good idea or not. Because her brain is slowed and not working. Would her smart self leave the car to dig out headlights? She doesn't know. And knows that she doesn't know.

She grunts and heaves herself up into a crouched position, moves her hands around to get some circulation going, and she tries the cell phone again but there is no signal. But she made the first call, right? Didn't she? She feels confused and slow, as if in a fog, but she remembers Anton telling her another story about how they located a drunk farm kid who had wandered off from his crushed truck but had made a call—something about an emergency locating ping. She likes that word, *ping*. And they had found and saved the kid, hadn't they?

She bends down, finds the leather gloves that are always in the glove compartment, wraps the space blanket around her. She doesn't want Satchmo to go running off in the blizzard— the least she can do is try to save the dog—and she crouches upright again. She thinks the truck might rock or move, and so she pushes her body forward, but it doesn't move in the slightest. It has been planted firmly sideways in the snow. She reaches up and clicks the ignition, enough to engage the automatic windows, and she depresses the driver's side window, but it gets stuck and so she grabs on to the pane and pushes and in comes the wind, howling. The dog starts whining and barking.

She sees a bag of old beef jerky at her feet, and bends down carefully in the small space to get it. She pushes some into her mouth and sprinkles the rest around the dog. "Stay!" she whispers.

She reaches out with both arms, braced on the frame of the door, and heaves herself up. The cold sucks the breath right out of her and burns her face. It takes her three tries—she's not as strong as she used to be, she's *old* for cripes sake—and finally she finds herself flopped on her belly on the truck's door. She's not so sure about this. This is the wrong thing to do. Stupid. But dying in the truck. She'd rather die outside. *Think, Renny, think.* Once she throws her feet over she'll land in snow. That will be fine. But she won't be able to get herself back in. And yet. The lights. If only the headlights were bright and clear—then someone could see her—there's a chance. She can blink them on and off and off and on. Someone, somewhere, will see her.

"It's a gamble," she pants. But still she can't decide. Go out or go back in? People die when they leave their cars. People die when they stay in their cars. She should decide quickly. She needs to make a decision and stick with it.

She's been hardening her heart—she can see that—for years. So that she wouldn't mourn Ben too deeply. She'd lost him when their daughter died. She'd lost him when she had blamed him for not tackling Ray in time. She'd lost him at the trial, when they watched Ray be sentenced and knew it would never be enough. She'd lost him when he withdrew into himself. She'd lost him when he built his own cabin on the opposite end of the ranch and, without a word, moved himself in. She'd lost him so many times already that perhaps she'd come to believe he was already dead.

The wind is smacking into her face, and it snaps her awake. She'll go out, shovel the headlights out, and then get back in. She'll move fast, one surefooted trip, and it will be her one act of courage, to at least give it a good try.

She slides off the door and into the snow. Immediately, she feels attacked. She can't fully open her eyes, she can't fully move forward in a straight line.

With head ducked and eyes open only a slit, she tries to step away from the truck. Satchmo is barking and trying to claw out and she yells *STAY* but is pretty sure all words get lost in the roar.

She thought Ben was going to die last night. She knew about the pink juice, she knew about the syringe, she assumed he had two syringes because a needle might break, as they often did. She knew he was capable of this, how he would want to go. She didn't know if he'd give himself the injection in bed or sneak out to the back pasture. All along, she figured he'd wait until spring, though, if not to see the flowers and the greening, but at least to make the burial easier. But after the cemetery today—was that today? Was that centuries ago?—after his weeping, after her weeping, she had assumed it was time. That he was going to take his life.

It hadn't occurred to her that he might have another plan. That he might want to face down Ray. That he might be planning to *kill* Ray. Could that be?

She stumbles through the snow, doubled over to keep the shards of snowflakes from piercing her skin. Funny, she thinks, how much snow can hurt, how the sheer force makes each bit pierce her skin.

In front of the truck, she reaches up to clean off the top headlight that is crusted over. Immediately a beam of light shoots over her into the cloudy light. She has done it. Then she bends down to shovel out—with her hands—the snow that has piled up around the one that is buried. Two beams of light. Two.

The sun is about to rise, or has perhaps even started, and until then, in the dark, she has this.

She remembers Jess, her quiet sullen granddaughter, who once whispered, *He's not dead yet, Grandma, he's in there*, and Renny had demanded, *What, what did you say?* and Jess had shrugged and refused to answer. She knew then that Jess was right.

She is panting now, and hot, and drops the blanket to the ground. Her skin feels as if it's overheating, as if it's on fire. She needs to get her clothes off. She doesn't know if Ben made it to Greeley before the storm or not. But once there, what would he do? Find Ray?

Maybe it was just instinct. Operating like she is now. A little uncertain, but by god, going to give it one strong try before going.

She wants so much to know what Ben was thinking, she wants so much to be the sort of woman who was warm enough to have curled next to Ben and listened to his plans, warm enough that he would have shared his secret. This one and all the other secret workings of his heart and mind. She wishes so much she could hold him one more time.

Don't be such a coward. That's what she wanted to tell Carolyn the other day, when she realized Carolyn was going to Mexico simply to escape. But now she understands. Ray's release has set loose an invisible and horrible wind. Ben will get caught in the wind, she knows it. Ben is perhaps the only one, in fact, who will stand up to that wind.

143

She wipes the tears. "I don't want to die yet," she says to the bright light that is now shining directly on her. Then she is on her knees, hunched over, convulsing into the snow.

She is so sorry. Sorry for her coldness, sorry for the way it has settled in her cells. Sorry to lose Ben. Sorry to lose herself.

BEN

He watches the snow change colors as the sky begins to lighten. Watches a branch of the cottonwood tree outside the window break from the weight, crack, and come down. Across the street there is a beautiful brick building, the old depot, and a huge metal grain silo. Oh, all the history and stories they contain.

He goes back into the bathroom, and he stares at himself in the mirror. He wants to see himself one last time. Blue eyes and curve of the nose and line of the jawbone that has been his for seven decades. There is Ben Cross. In all his versions. Boy and young man and man and middle-aged man and older man. There is his soul and his body and his mind and all that is him. Staring back at him.

From the bathroom, he hears the ding of a door. Inside his own brain, he hears the roar of water, a dam breaking. It's true he's sweating. It's true he's scared. He's been this way before, breaking a horse or facing down a bull. He knows he can weather it.

Rachel, dark hair, pajamas, clinging to his back, hugging him tight around the neck. Despair, then. Daughter in her coffin, the impossibility of that little girl now laid out, dark long hair still at her side.

Renny, holding the baby and another baby and Renny's eyes were sparkling, then, sparkling with water. And the life ran with water, greened the fields and his heart. The water trickled into the cells of his daughters and they grew and he would walk the fields with them, irrigating or checking cows, and it was spring, always spring, always the best time for water, always water.

He looks around, confused. This bathroom. This is not his bathroom. It is not a bathroom he remembers.

Then he hears the voices outside again. He hears a particular voice outside the bathroom. It is a friendly, easygoing voice that says, *Hey, man,* and it is the voice that has been speaking to him in letters and then in his own head. It is a voice that has been arguing with him, pleading his case, making excuses, whining.

He remembers. Now that he has heard the voice. The remembering room in his brain has sparked alive.

Two syringes are filled, in the pocket of his Carhartt jacket. He had his gun, but now he does not. He must get the syringe right. He must be careful and fast, all at one time. It will be the greatest act of his life.

His hands are sweaty—he's so hot! He wants to take off this jacket—the bathroom heater is going full blast—but he must keep it on—he must accomplish this. Still, he keeps his hands in his pockets, fingers of each hand curled around a syringe that is now filled to capacity. He needs to take his hand out of his pocket to open the bathroom door. And yet he can't. He stands there, in the bathroom, and waits.

Go slow. Take it easy. Make sure you know what you're doing, see.

He was always saying that to his girls. When they learned to ride horses, give cattle shots, stick their hands in a cow's rear end to pregnancy-check.

Go slow. Take it easy. Make sure you know what you're doing, see.

His chest hurts, his arm hurts. There's a heavy pressure in his chest. Something is wrong with him, he knows it. But he can still take it easy, be careful. And that is how he removes his hand from his pocket, opens the bathroom door, and walks out to face the man who is turning, thirty degrees, forty-five degrees, ninety degrees to face him. Like a math problem.

Ray. Ray who looks the same, nearly, with dark hair and dark eyes and a face reddened by life and sun and broken blood vessels, Ray who stands there, clearly nervous and watchful, Ray who stands there like a man struggling to find the bravery to face the consequences of what he has wrought. Ray who is succeeding—just barely—in that bravery, and Ben, for a moment, hesitates, because he knows how hard it is to be brave. The woman who has been selling someone a ticket has grown quiet and the world is quiet and the snowstorm outside is quiet. But quiet is not exactly what he needs now. He needs the rage of before, the constant battle in his mind, the arguing and pleading with Ray that lives as part of his brain now. And indeed, in the distance, he can hear it. *Out, Ray. You coward, Ray. You fake. You bastard. Don't give me excuses. Don't give me reasons. Give me my daughter back. Give me my time back on earth, the time that was beautiful and full. The time before you.*

"Ben. Ben Cross." Ray pulls himself up tall like a brave man, but a bead of sweat meanders down the side of his face, a tremor visible in his jaw. "It's good . . . it's more than good . . . for you to come. Although you picked a hellofa night." He clears his throat and Ben studies him. To know the measure of a man. Such a fine, small distinction. That is what Renny used to tell him. That she'd fallen in love with him because he could mark the measure of a man. Ben has always believed that you do this by noting what's in a man's eyes the instant you look at them, before the real self has time to put up a mask and conceal and act out whatever particular story. For a moment, if you glance into the eye of a human before they have the chance to do this, you can see what's real.

What he sees: A charm, but not a core.

What he sees: An actor and a bully.

What he sees: Jess and Billy and the rest of his family, with this man always on the periphery. Always pushing in.

What he sees: He's never killed a man, but if he does, he will have birthed peace.

What he sees: That perhaps this is a sin, perhaps it is wrong.

What he sees: He needs to decide one way or another and hold true to that decision.

He looks once again at Ray's eyes, and he sees fear and he sees a flinch, a flinch that means that Ray has judged his own self as less than he could be. Ray is disappointed in himself. Ray sees at least a little bit of what Ben does.

Ben walks up to Ray, as if to hug him, and he does hug him, and Ray holds him and says, "Ben. Oh, Ben . . ."

As Ben backs away from the hug he asks himself, *You sure? Be sure*, and his mind says, *Yes, sure*, and he takes the syringe from his right pocket. He holds it in his right hand and looks to thrust it into Ray's chest but there is a leather jacket there, unzipped, but still covering the heart. He knows he'll break the needle. He knows this. His hands do it of their own. They reach out, move the jacket to the side, run down Ray's breastbone, move to the left, palpate the ribs—right as Ray is wondering what Ben is doing, touching his heart, and then perhaps comprehending and moving backward—yes, there!—right below the lower right rib, pointing up, he will get the liver.

The poison will slowly spread in this way, throughout Ray's body like water. Through the valleys and watersheds of the body. Through the channels and irrigation ditches. Through the meandering tissue and juicy flesh.

Ben's palm finds the plunger and he is strong enough to stay with Ray, who is bucking around, this is like riding a horse, and with one hand he holds the syringe and with the other palm he depresses the plunger, slowly, slowly—it requires all his strength, his hands hurt and his forearms ache—and the thick liquid disappears into Ray's body. But then Ray is thrashing, pushing Ben's arm away. Ben remembers the gun. *This* is why he wanted the gun, to have the room to make a mistake, to put down an animal that was suffering.

And what is this? A person standing near him. Like an angel. He hears her say, "It's the right thing you're doing, Ben. I can't help you, but you don't need help. You can do it." And Ben guides the needle back a little, repositions, and pushes the plunger the rest of the way.

Ray starts up a scream. Like a dying horse. Like a dying man. Like fear. Like a human being, every human being, left on a beautiful planet with no god and no hope.

Courage is fear that has said its prayers. Please forgive me if I've done wrong. He doesn't know if he thinks this or if he hears it, but it helps him continue. Perhaps it takes only a fraction of a second, but time slows and he sees each slow decrease in the ccs, fraction by fraction, as if it were an entire lifetime.

Then the needle bends, and then it snaps.

"What the—what the—oh, Jesus, that stings! What was that?" Ray is making a silent-noise now, like the horse when he finally shot it, at the moment the bullet took hold. Like Renny in one of their fights. Like Rachel's silence in the seconds before she died. Like his heart.

The thing is, Ben thinks, is that Ray's existence on the planet was always going to haunt. Always going to hurt. Some gut instinct that he trusts. Ray has never really *been* sorry. Always selfish in this fundamental way. He will take more then he will ever give.

Ben turns to see the girl. He can see now that the angel looks like his granddaughter, only she looks different. Different hair. Different color. Is it Jess?

"Shhh," she tells him. "I just wanted to be with you. I didn't want you to be alone."

He cries out. A bellow of thanks and of pain, to the universe and at Ray and at the people who hurt children and the people who hurt land and the very fact of his disease and the very fact he is dying. The screaming of Ray and the howl of Ben roar like water and ricochet around the small room like a beast, and now the woman is sobbing too and the sirens are far away.

Had he gotten the heart, it would have killed Ray fast. But now it will take a bit and Ray will be mobile for a moment and Ben knows he needs to run. Ray is coming at him now, his face angry and red, the same face—the same face!—that he saw running in his house right after his daughter!—and the face that once said *goddamn bitch can't leave me*, and the face that Ben does not want haunting his family.

Ben stares at his legs because he needs them to move. They are the legs of an old man, which surprises him. How did that happen? Gray pants over bone and thin skin. How did they dry out so much? But the muscles flex and the bones move and he is running. Out the front door, which jingles behind him, right out into the blinding snow. His heart gallops. The cold is astonishing. *Two for two. Two for two.* He must be outside, he must. As he gallops along—his legs gallop with his heart—he turns to the right, toward the old depot, and takes out the second syringe from the left pocket and takes the cap from the tip and throws it to the ground.

Now he must move fast. Through the snow, which sends him tumbling down. He's never seen the likes of a winter like this. He rises up, stumbles, falls, rises again. Ahead is the depot and the silo and a cottonwood. The cottonwood is hibernating like a bear now but soon enough full of sap and greenery and he stands below it, turns to see the police cars pulling up, screaming sirens, turns to see Ray staggering through the snow after him, and his very movement will speed up the spread of poison, this Ben knows.

Ben turns away from them all, and the snow is falling beautifully now, in large warm flakes and the sun is breaking through the clouds. There is the smallest little area of blue sky above the depot, above the silo, above the tree. It is there that he will ascend.

He wonders how his life looks to the stars. He wonders if the universe has remembered the planet and her people. He wonders if, even, the earth *is* the remembering room of all that is.

He would have liked to die on the ranch. But he can imagine it, conjure it into being, and he does now. There is the line of willows, bright red and orange against the snow, becoming redder as the weather warms, nearly so bright as to hurt his eyes. There is the bald eagle flying over. And there is the snow melting and the first greening of the grass, and the small crocuses by the house turning out their first curl of green, and then the first bloom of color. There is the sky and the mountains and the green pasture and the spread of his beautiful ranch. There are the first rainfalls of spring and the huge thunderstorms of summer. The aspens will first have their catkins, then they will unfurl their first small heart-shaped leaves.

He wishes he had written a note to the others, for it seems like something he would have wanted to do. The note he wrote himself, that was a gift he must now have the courage to accept.

He stays facing this direction so he can see snow and blue sky, and he shrugs off his jacket, all the while looking up. One last time, he looks around. He sees the girl in the distance, standing like an alert deer, watching him. He takes the syringe from his pocket, holds it with one hand and palpates his ribs with the other, and stares at it for a moment, at the beautiful liquid, the water that promises peace.

RENNY

And so finally at this last moment, Ben has deeply communicated with her. She feels her mind becoming what his was. Slow. Frozen. He has come to her after all, shown her what it was like to be him, stuck with a mind that is failing. Communicated at last. It is much scarier than she thought it would be, and oh, how he has handled this with courage, handled the rising, choking fear with a calm bravery.

As she hangs on the truck's door, she imagines voices. Imagines colors. Imagines lights. She tries to pull herself up and over the side of the truck, but she simply cannot. She falls. Feels her body convulse. The wind. It's screaming and whistling like a creature that is alive, like a siren. Her body convulses again, and then again.

She stands—or thinks she does—and puts her arms on the truck window and tries to pull herself up, again, but it can't be done. It can't be done. She can either sit in the snow or lean against the truck, and so she tries to do this, to prop herself upright. She is struggling against something. The wind that feels like arms, pushing her this way and that. She should have found a way to protect them all—Ben and Carolyn and the grandchildren and herself—a little better.

If she can keep her mind active, going over the same litany of things she used to ask Ben, perhaps she will stay alive. She closes her eyes and thinks of each person in the family. How Carolyn will take care of Ben, and how, when things get bad enough, Carolyn will have the toughness and the sense to move him to an assisted living place.

She thinks of Jack. Wonders if he'll become a lawyer. Pictures him roping a steer, which he was good at, but never did enjoy. She knew early on that he'd become a city kid, which was fine by her. Although, she realizes now, she never quite told him that.

She wonders if Leanne will stay single for a long time. Leanne has career in mind, and less mothering instinct than any of them. Good. She'll do something else with her life, and be very sturdy and bossy about it.

She wonders about Billy and what sort of man he will turn out to be, and hopes he doesn't become an oil-rig worker and get hooked on meth. But perhaps he will find someone to love and will live an honest and decent life, working the land. She can easily imagine him gathering eggs from chickens.

She wonders about Jess, and wonders if Jess and Ben share some particular genetic code. They are so much alike, see the world with so much quiet stillness, like an evening sky, and she has never understood it. Perhaps she has unfairly disliked them for it, because it is hard to appreciate things you do not understand. Perhaps the fault was only hers all along.

The dog is whining, then barking. Or at least she dreams it. She's so blissful and tired. Good dog. The rising sun gives a weak slant of light through the clouds, and she stares up at the gray sky, one small patch of morning-lit blue.

There are many things she should have done. Told someone where she was going. Told Carolyn and Leanne and Jess and Jack and Billy good-bye. Put the ranch in a conservation easement. Donated some money to the Alzheimer's Association or some group that helps people die. Put a new cover on her book, one that read THE DAMN INTERESTING STORY OF RENNY AND BEN.

One story in particular she should have put down. It comes to her now, like a dream, only not. It's more like reality curved in on itself. It's happening to her again. The spring after Rachel died, after Ben had moved out back. A cow was having trouble giving birth, she'd called for him and the vet, and when Ben came and put his hand inside the mother and pulled on the tail of the calf inside, there was no movement. Dead inside the mother. They'd need to do a fetotomy. And while they waited for the vet, Renny and Ben stood in the mucky corral, spattered in blood, and Ben had pointed out the bald eagle that had been hanging out above the river. She wanted to tell him, then, that she let the dogs sleep with her on the bed, so that there was some weight and warmth beside her. She wanted to ask him if he did the same, and if he responded with a yes, she wanted to make a joke about how the dogs' situation, at least, had improved since their separation. But when she turned to say something, she saw that he was staring in the direction of the river at the blue sky with some thought that has stilled him, and he was blanketed in light snow, a dusting of white settled on his hair and jacket, and she did not speak. When the vet arrived with his black vinyl bag, and took out the long wire strung between two metal handles, she tried not to watch. But she couldn't help it. How he looped the wire in a circle in his palm, closed his fingers over it, and pushed his fist into the cow. How he rubbed the cow's hind legs with his left hand as he worked inside her with his right, and hummed a long conversation to her. *You'll feel better soon, mama mama mama sweet mama girl, bet you're hurting but it's almost over, sweet old mama.* How she took those words to be personally directed at her. How she knew he was looping the wire behind the hind quarter and was going to saw the calf apart inside the mother, so as to help her live. There is Ben and the vet and they alternated pulling, the *whir* of the wire, and Renny stood at the head of the cow, consoling her. The cow, she could tell, was straining once more with this feeling of something moving inside her, and her ears flicked backward at this new sound coming from her rear end.

Ben talked about the calf they would graft on. And she knew, from his face, that he felt sick. In all their years of ranching, they'd had to do this only twice before, and they found it unacceptable. And she saw his face pale even more when the tension of the line met the bone of the unborn calf's leg, and again when the vet reached inside the cow and pulled out the calf's hind quarter, severed from the groin, and even more when it slushed out in a waterfall of blood at Ben's feet.

The cow tried to turn, then, but the halter kept her head in place, and Renny was there anyway, scratching her ears and blocking her view. She kept her eyes on Ben, then, so she didn't have to see the chunk of calf. At first, Ben's face was so familiar that she couldn't really *see* Ben. Who was this man? This human being? She had to concentrate. Note that his hair was now nearly white. That he'd cut himself shaving just below the jawline. How his eyes looked soft and calm, despite the fact that he hated what he was doing. Her knowledge of him was so limited, so incomplete. So she turned to the cow, instead.

"Just get through this, Mama," she'd said into the cow's ear as she scratched it. "I know just how you feel. Carolyn was easy. But that Rachel. I thought she was ripping me apart. The plight of mothers, I tell you."

Then the rest of the calf was dislodged and a waterfall of blood and yellow fluid came with her next strain. The cow shifted her weight, then tensed. The rest of the calf slithered from her in a pool of membranes and blood and flopped to the ground. A blue tongue hung from the side of a small mouth, eyes open in a dead stare. Guts and the spinal cord protruded from the back part of the calf, and steam rose, and blood pooled into the snow. The cow tried to turn and thrashed wildly when she could not break free of her halter. She was trying to get to her calf, to lick it, and that simple need is what broke Renny's heart.

When the vet left, Ben skinned the calf and tied the hide to another calf in need of a mother. Renny finally untied the cow, stepped away, and watched as the cow turned to sniff the calf, her nose running across the pieces of hide. Then she moved to where the blood has soaked into the ground and her nose hovered there. She considered the calf for a moment, sniffed it again, regarded it suspiciously. It stepped toward her and let out a meek bawl. Ben and Renny stood quiet, hoping. The cow moved forward then, slid her tongue over the calf's face and ears, and stood still as it teetered toward her bag of milk and sucked.

Renny and Ben smiled at each other. "At least," Renny had said, "we can still do that." Meaning: smile. Meaning: save a thing or two.

They began to clean up the mess, and Ben told her that he'd dump the pieces of the calf beyond his cabin, near the gully, in the brush. The dogs wouldn't dig through the mass of sticks to get to the calf, and besides, the body would be frozen to the ground soon, then covered by snow. And then they spoke of their dead daughter. The only time they truly did. About how she was bones now, and that fact broke each breath of each day. They spoke of how, by the time everything melted, the calf would have decayed. It's amazing, they said, how a life—laughter, arguments, little arms reaching out for a hug—how everything ends up as clean bones.

Before they parted ways—he to the job of disposing of the calf and to his cabin, she to the farmhouse—he had told her to wait. He'd wiped his hands on his jeans, inspected them, and reached out to brush a wisp of hair from Renny's face. She had started to say something, but then stopped, but she knew he understood. That she had no words that could begin to close the space but that she loved him anyway. He nodded his understanding and offered a sad smile in return. They had turned, then, each ducking into the swirling snow. Her heart shining, for a bit, from the soft touch of his hand on her hair, his kind eyes on hers.

She is there, on that winter day. The past has circled round to this moment. It is a hallucination, of course, she hears her brain whisper. The last hold of her reason-filled brain slipping away. What the brain does in hypothermia. Or perhaps not. Perhaps she is in that moment again. The woodenness turns to warmth.

What's gone is gone. Her heart is flipping around. Like a dying fish. Except a fish that doesn't mind. Only the heart cares what it's doing, but not the rest of her. She's never felt so calm. So peaceful. If she had the energy, or if she cared more, she would tear off her clothes, she's so hot. It must be the sun, burning through the clouds to get her. *It's probably Ben*, she thinks, trying to warm her. *That was very nice of him,* she thinks. Very kind for him to come for her in that swirling snowstorm after all. To say that they didn't save the calf, and they didn't save their daughter, but they saved another calf, and they saved the mother, and they could save each other now.

How kind of him. How kind.

IV.

"*We two alone will sing like birds in the cage:*
When thou dost ask me blessing, I'll kneel down,
And ask of thee forgiveness: so we'll live,
And pray, and sing, and tell old tales, and laugh
And talk upon's the mystery of things,
And we'll wear out, packs and sects of great ones
That ebb and flow by the moon."

—WILLIAM SHAKESPEARE

King Lear (act 5, scene 3)

JESS

Pretend, if you will, that this is a story, and that I should be the one to tell it, and that it ends like this: Much of the wind-whipped snow melted rapidly, octave by octave, and then the poured and patterned ice underneath melted as well, and the earth was stunned with an influx of seeping water and it gurgled and muddied and transformed into a ripe-smelling soaked mess and, in stops and starts, dutifully absorbed all this water, until, finally, as we knew it would, offered up a slight greening, a twinge of soggy color. There are still rings of snow in the shade, and the north-facing slopes of the foothills remain dusted in white, and there are still ruts of mud on every dirt county road, and there is still the decay and dried grasses of winter. But you understand how things change rapidly, that one good moment of observation will reveal this to you. This one good moment of observation is all we really have in the world and it is called love.

During this past week, the irrigation ditches melted in pops and zings of twinging ice, the sound echoing across the farm. During this time, the geese and then the meadowlarks returned, the cattle of neighboring ranches dropped their first calves into the snow and they now stand, wobbly kneed, regarding the world with startled white-faced wonder. The owls by the river went to nest, and, as always, it is nearly impossible to see them and it takes a trained and patient eye. The horses, on the other hand, are often easy to spot, out galloping just for the fun of it, running to the edge of a fence and then bunching to a halt.

During this time, the willows swelled into a bright and pure orange.

It is only now, gathered here for the funeral, in the same field that Ben walked by every day, it is only now, you understand, that we can stop and see ourselves as the universe might: culpable and proud.

Ben was the one who stole the pink juice from the vet.

Ruben knew it. Saw Ben do it. Pretended, as he had to do, that he did not.

Renny knew it. Found the note that Ben was always carrying around, the one that reminded him where he'd hidden it.

Carolyn knew it. She found the bottle in the barn when she was putting away the saddles. She barely had the strength to leave it. It was she who was most troubled and it was she who would have told the authorities, and she knew it, and so she left on a vacation to Mexico. But first she broke her own stove—tore at the wires!—in order to spend as much time over there, busy but watchful, as she could. It was the wires that clued me in, and the way her eyes darted to the barn, uncertain.

And I knew it. Because, you see, Ben told me. Many times. Because each time, he'd forget he had already told me, and so he would tell me again. Always, we were playing cards, out back in the cabin. And he'd say: *Jess, there's something I gotta do, see.* And so you understand that I was the only one who knew that he also had Ray in mind. I wasn't sure he'd actually *do* it. If what he was talking about was only a hope. Or a dream. Or just a I-would-do-this-if-I-could type of narrative. But some days I felt certain he would. That my own grandfather was going to kill my stepfather and then himself. That he had a reason, and that we went over this reason many times. You understand, perhaps, what a hard story this has been to tell.

★

Pretend, if you will, that this is a story, and that it ends like this: Renny's hospital stay had its moments of fear. The rewarming process was not easy, physically or emotionally. They use blankets with fluid pumped through them. In this way, the fluid can be gradually heated so that the body, too, can be gradually heated. Too much warming at once can kill you. The heart cannot take the rush of cold blood that comes at it with a sudden warming. Heart failure, they say. Explosion of the heart. If it happens too fast. The heart, they say, crashes around, trying to beat. If it's warmed slowly, it can adjust. The same, in many ways, goes for Renny.

When released from the hospital, she said that she would probably never feel fully warm again. And still, I know that her feet and arms often tingle and she says she often feels wooden and sore, although she has never once complained. Instead, she put in the paperwork to the county, the Authorization for Final Disposition, which is required for burial on private property. It took seven days, which is how long it took everyone to get gathered. That's how long it took to get the autopsy and investigation done—to determine both the cause of death and also to take a slice of brain to confirm Alzheimer's and to indicate that it appeared his heart was going anyway. That's how long it took to make the coffin, to make the necessary preparations.

I stand in the field, hands jammed in my pockets, and consider: It's good to see my family slowly start to right themselves after the initial blast and internal swaying-back that the news of Ben's death caused. Even if many of us knew it was coming. It's good to see that there is a kind of healing with Renny and that she comes out of her daze.

She has, for instance, declared the equinox a good day to bury Ben on the ranch, not because of any metaphorical meaning, but because it's practical and *makes sense*, which means that Renny has found her dry core again. The ground can be dug up, no one is busy with planting yet, everyone is able to gather, and because she can move without too much pain again.

But she is changed: I can see it. The way she carries herself, tilting her head and considering the fields or the person or the sky, as if she is considering it all anew. She is in a very fragile position right now. Her heart is changed. And you understand that I mean this literally. When she started to regain warmth and consciousness, in the hospital, it's then that she was in the most danger. As her core warmed, her body allowed the warm blood to flow to the extremities. That, the doctors told me, flushed a surge of cold blood toward the heart. Cold blood can kill.

Which is to say: The warming of the heart must be gradual. Like a melting of the spring. Or it can kill. Which is why I'll be around to help her in this process. I helped Ben freeze and I will help Renny melt.

I finger the pink Valentine's Day card that I have folded in my pocket. Construction paper, light pink, soft fibers of paper.

It contains the last thing Ben ever wrote, the last thing Renny wrote, although she'll have time to add to her words.

I finger it and watch her boss people around. Renny will still want to maintain her position that I don't speak because I'm stupid and that I will, of course, become pregnant and a drug addict. That I am too much like my grandfather, too calm and watchful to be of much use. I watch her say these words now, at the funeral, and I love her for her particular brand of love and her tenacity and her power. I wink at her and say: I'll help you find another way to love me.

★

My mother, of course, did not receive an Authorization for Final Disposition. She was just disposed, at the cemetery in town, which is where I saw Ben and Renny. I had just driven there myself and put down river rocks and then taken a walk through the tombstones, which is when I saw them stumble through the snow with pink roses. I watched from behind a tree as Ben lost his temper, as Anton guided them home, as Renny soothed.

I knew that the time had come. If it was going to come at all, well, then this was it. So I followed them home in my truck. Followed Ben back into town. Followed Ben to the Greyhound station. Disguised myself a bit, mainly by demeanor, because, you know, we recognize people by the very way they hold themselves, and much can be achieved by simply changing the way we move our bodies. Although I also had a wig, left over from some school costume long ago. I helped him get the ticket. Watched him get on the bus. Decided at the last moment to go ahead and get on myself. *Tell ya what I'm going to do, see.* Activity manifests the essence. No one wants to die alone. But

169

I kept to myself and left him largely on his own. This was his decision, after all, and he wanted to be the only one culpable. I did get to run over and hold his hand for a moment, though, before the police pushed me away.

You understand I was not the only one, though, to bear witness. To watch with careful love and attention.

Ruben, for instance, had stood in the post office, confused and startled by Renny's slap. During this pause, he'd happened to look down into the trash can. Recognized the name Ray Steele. Pulled the letter out of the trash. Determined that he'd keep it, in case Renny ever wanted it back. When everyone started searching for Ben, it slowly dawned on him like it must have dawned on Renny. Somehow, all this mess—Ben missing, and then Renny missing—had to do with Ray. So he called Anton. Anton contacted the Greeley Police, who were responding to blizzard emergencies, and who sent out the call for Renny's truck, and who got to the bus station just a moment after Ben injected the juice. This is important only for a small reason, perhaps, which is that by the time two men were dying in Greeley, and Renny was close to dying in Ault, there were blankets about them, someone holding their hands, others taking pulses and touching foreheads. And to me, that's somehow comforting. That the two men died with the sure knowledge that humanity was trying to come through for them.

Oh, Ben: I would sit with him and I would tell him in my silence that he was very real, and very alive, and very deserving of love. I hope he heard me. I hope his heart heard the water in mine.

★

The final disposition permit papers are pinned down by two river rocks on the picnic table, rustling and flapping. Ben Cross is inside a homemade wooden casket made out of beetle-kill pine trees, the wood naturally stained gray-blue with the fungus those beetles leave behind. Eddie and Anton made it, even nailed it shut with old handmade nails that have been found on the place, on Hell's Bottom Ranch. Otherwise known as a slice of heaven. As people around here say.

The coffin sits next to a hole dug in the ground by all the men yesterday, shovels still stabbed into the mounds of dirt, waiting for the work of filling back in. Satchmo is digging a hole in one of the piles, the dirt flying behind her, tail wagging.

The sky is so thin. The sky is defined by what it doesn't have, which is water. It's so weightless and pure that I know Ben's soul could easily pass through. It is a sky that is descending from daytime hours to the start of dusk. The moon is rising. *L'heure bleue.* The blue hour. The time of the souls. Sometimes I wish I could notice the beauty less, because I'll tell you (although I am guessing you already know), such beauty can shatter one's heart.

★

So here we are, under such a sky: Del and Carolyn and Renny have put out tables and chairs by the orange willows, which are still circled in the remnants of unmelted snow.

People are starting to park on the rutted road or they're walking from the house if they don't think their cars have enough clearance. Ben's path has never had so much company. Everyone is carrying buckets of KFC from town, or casseroles, or Jell-O desserts, holding their coats and jackets to them since the wind has picked up. It almost makes me cry, seeing this. The absurdity and beauty and weirdness of Jell-O. Of death. Of the human heart.

It's still cold, quite cold, and so we've all lugged out enough lumber to have a bonfire, which is where I'm sitting now, feeding the fire and being mesmerized by the flames, as all people for all time have been. I have on my jeans and a black sweater and I have painted my fingernails orange, because this was the color that my mother had painted my nails, and hers, the very day she died. It's a tribute to her, and to Grandpa Ben, who liked the willows. It's a prayer, even, that perhaps my mother is welcoming my grandfather and maybe even my stepfather into the Great Mysterious Beyond or whatever comes next.

I watch. It's true that I am the final record keeper of this family. That is my job. And when Renny asks what I'm going to make of my life, I'll tell her I don't know, but that it will ebb and flow, and at the very least, that I do know I am the record keeper, and that this is a true story, and it goes like this:

★

The individuals here matter very much.

For example. There is Ruben. Pausing for a breath, and, I know, trying to come out from underneath both his guilt and his relief. Ben pulled it off, which is what Ruben knows Ben wanted. He'd thought the pink juice was for Ben only, hadn't envisioned this other possibility, and wonders if he would have turned away and pretended not to notice had he known otherwise. He supposes he would have, truth be told. He supposes he's happy that Ben took Ray. Ray being the sort of person that frequently hit a child named Jess, and this Jess is now turning into a woman, and who is too young, and whom he is thus working hard not to love. Although. It's an odd thing to do to love. He didn't go asking for this emotion, and it annoys him it just arrived. He needs to expel it. Or, at the very least, maneuver it so that the place it occupies inside is comfortable, or if not comfortable, then bearable. He does not know yet. I'll tell him on my birthday, the day I become less of a girl and more of a woman, and it still won't be quite right, but perhaps in a few years it will be. I'll let him know that I know. That I love him back. He and his way with animals. His calm healing. His sharp eyes. He is, of course, beautiful, and although I have no faith in the longevity of love or have any silly notions of needing to be saved, I would, in fact, not mind growing up with him for a while. I will also tell him that I know of the pink juice. Because Ben told me. Told me that Ruben looked away, on purpose, and that they caught one another's eye. And because he shouldn't have to live alone with that secret forever.

There is Anton. Being Anton, he has the volunteer fire truck tank parked in the field, because although it's spring it's still gusty. While it's likely that any spark would dissolve into the cold wetness (like a soul, burning bright and then dampened and dead) there is the possibility that the opposite will happen. Colorado has already had too many wildfires, and will continue to burn. You also understand that he is just now processing what he knows. That he had been making inquiries on behalf of Renny and Ben and because he once loved Rachel, back when they were in high school, and still felt a certain duty. You understand that these inquires led him to understand that a certain Ray Steele had been in communication with a man named Luce. Money was needed, after all, to start life anew. Money from meth. It was only a hunch. And now he knows that Luce was on that same bus. Later arrested for stealing a gun. For possession of meth. Arrested because Anton had been following the story of Ray, which led him to Luce, which led the police to Luce. That Luce will soon be heading to the same prison that once housed Ray.

There's Billy. Walking toward Ruben in an offer to help with the last of the firewood. There's also Del. And Leanne and Jack, my stepsiblings, or my cousins, depending on how you view it. When I saw them, Jack immediately put me in a headlock and gave me a head rub, and I punched him back and leaned into his arms for a while because Jack has always been like that, willing to let me communicate in that roughhouse way. He seems to need fewer words.

There's Violet, Eddie, the folks from the Alzheimer's Association, including Esme, who is nice, and a guy named Zach who seems to put his arm around Renny a lot in a protective kind of gesture. His wife, I hear, has just moved into assisted care.

There's the pregnant lady. The waitress at the place where we got stopped in the snowstorm. She'd read the story in the paper, about Ben and Ray, and she asked if she could be there when Ben was buried.

There are the ranchers. The people from the Presbyterian church. The Stitch Club ladies, who are the women who have been meeting since forever to make quilts and gossip. There are a lot of people, really, that one individual life touches.

There is Carolyn. The mother that raised me. Not knowing that I know. Thinking that she carries this burden herself.

There is Renny. Thinking, I know, of the hospital. The same one where she'd given birth to Carolyn and then Rachel. And where Carolyn gave birth to her two. And where Rachel was taken before they declared her dead. And where Ben and Ray were brought for autopsy. She's thinking of me visiting her there. Arriving as soon as the Greyhound got me back into town. The first on the scene. Holding her hand as she came to. Her trying to shake my hand away, me refusing to let it go. Me delighted to see her reduced to calm and reasonable behavior. Even if by drugs. How she slapped my hand away, but how I took it back up again, which is a simple motion that Ben used to do. How Renny had said to me: *Two for two. Ben kept saying that. I thought he meant that he was dying twice. First his mind, then his body. But he meant two births—his two daughters—and two deaths—Ray and himself. I didn't know that that's what he meant.*

I did, I told her. *I did.*

And she said: *You were with him?*

And I said: *Yes. I could feel him going, and it was peaceful. We'll have to keep remembering that. We'll have to put it in the remembering room of our heads. You have hypothermia. Your bones and joints will hurt. Your skin will hurt. But you will recover.*

And when I left, I placed the journal on her stomach. THE SAD STORY OF RENNY AND BEN. And when I came back to get her from the hospital, one word had been crossed out. It now read THE DAMN INTERESTING STORY OF RENNY AND BEN.

Here we all are, in this story of ours.

★

Such events, of course, bring out a certain type of honest hope and honest fear. I hear it in the chatter all around me. If I close my eyes and focus, I can hear a little symphony of parts:

Generous thoughts are hard to come by today, when it
    comes to Ray—
I'd much rather complain than count my blessings—
This wind better die down—

Speaking of, there was a man in Mexico selling these
   kites . . .
—I think it's a myth that Eskimo elders put themselves out
   on ice floes—
I can't make it through this funeral without a better coat—
It's pigeon disease, the horses get it from the dirt—
—No, he didn't lose his vet license, it's under investigation,
   I hope they let him off, him being so young and all. He's
   just got to keep his meds locked up—
—The Alzheimer's Association's official stance is that
   anonymous testing should be available. We've argued
   that—
She's going to end up pregnant and on drugs—
Now, Renny, it's possible she's tuned *in* —
—Well, *look* at her, all quiet like that. Where *is* she? In her
   mind, I mean? Although, maybe. You never know.
Tell me again, Renny—
—I think we all learn not to feel loneliness anymore. We
   get distracted. We distract our whole lives away.
—Occasionally one is wise to the ways of the universe. Gut
   instinct, intuition, sixth sense. I now know, for instance,
   that I was being saved at the exact same time Ben was
   dying. I almost felt—I can't really say this, can I? It
   makes me sound like a woo-woo nutcase, that I felt his
   arms around me, heaving me out of the snow, pulling
   me toward warmth, a voice saying *there now, hang on.*
   Sounds like a bunch of New Agey hippie crap, doesn't
   it? And yet.
It's been proven that mountain views are good for the
   brain.
But mountains don't pay taxes. This community needs—
Some towns don't *want* to be developed—

—So Renny is going to move back to the cabin? Del and
    Carolyn are inheriting?—

—And Anton is buying that southern edge? To pay the
    taxes?

—It's a good solution. Estate taxes . . .

I just never would have thought—

I'll be damned, something called a contemplative dying
    movement?

—They said she looked dead—

That can be common. Frozen folks can look dead, even
    for hours, and still come alive. There's that rewarming
    adage: "They aren't dead until they are *warm* and dead."

—It's a lucky thing, for sure.

—I sure like what he used to say about hope. His brain
    wouldn't have gotten better. He knew that. He knew
    that it's wrong to hope for what isn't going to happen.

—She just quit talking after Rachel died. And it got worse
    when Ray was let out of prison—

—Poor Rachel. This funeral makes me miss her all over
    again.

We need to focus on the living—

We need to focus on the planet.

It must have been an ugly death for Ray. Ben got him in the
    liver. Agonal breathing—

Ben had got himself in the heart. Quick, peaceful.

—Just like an animal that doesn't get put down quite right.
    If it had been one of their animals, Ben would have fol-
    lowed up with a gun; he hated to see things suffer.

Ben wouldn't have done *that* on purpose—

Oh, I know.

He would have tried—

I know it.

It's not an easy thing—

Oh, I know it—

She's not allowing any paper plates or Lipton tea. Says it's all crap. Warm and dead, eh? I like that. Plenty of people are cold-hearted and alive.

—Oh, that Renny. One can try to prepare for her, but one will fail.

—Well, I don't like Lipton tea either. Let's be honest. Who does?

★

I watch as Renny prepares for this final moment. She's wearing her down coat with rips and duct-tape patches and hiking boots. This is pretty much how everyone is dressed; it is simply too muddy and sloppy to consider anything else. She gets everyone seated and quiet, except the dog, whom she commands to sit, but who instead runs from person to person to get food and attention. Most people are sitting on hay bales or benches, china plates balanced on their knees and a beer in their hands. Renny announces that she'd like everyone to say a short thing or two, a memory perhaps, and that she'd like to go last.

Anton recalls the time that Ben ate peanut butter that he had found in an old hunting cabin, but it turns out that the peanut butter had d-CON mixed in to put on mousetraps, so they had to take him to the emergency room.

Ruben tells a few stories of he and Ben saving animals together, and Ben's sure and quick hand when it came to swiping gunk from newborn calves' mouths or his sure-footed calmness when putting down an animal that was suffering, which makes us all think of his final act of putting down his own animal self.

Violet blushes and recounts the time that she had first moved to town and bought the grocery; she'd seen Ben for the first time and hoped he wasn't married, but then, nodding at Renny, after the initial disappointment, she was glad to call both Renny and Ben friends.

Eddie recounts the time they went up to save a herd of cattle from the Rattlesnake Fire, as it was called, and haul all the animals down the mountain in their trailers, in the dust and smoke and chaos.

Leanne talks about the time she saw Ben get slammed into a fence by a bull and how everyone stood over him, waiting to see if he would breathe, and it was then that she loved him most, just that one strange moment.

Jack says something about how it was Ben who taught him to ride figure eights across the field.

Billy recounts how Grandpa Ben would sit with him, just sit, after Rachel died.

The pregnant woman from the truck stop tells about sleeping next to Ben in the booth and the blizzard outside. She knew he was confused but figured he was just tired. She wants to apologize for not calling the police, that she would feel better if she could publicly apologize for not doing more, but that she'd just been so tired, too. What with the crowd, the blizzard, and being pregnant and all, she'd found it hard to think. She also says that Ben had changed her life, that he had warned her about hope, that it could sometimes freeze you up and make you not take action, because you just hoped things would get better when in fact they would not, and so after that snowstorm, she broke up with her boyfriend, who had a gambling addiction and was losing money as fast as she could make it. She had moved into her brother's house so she can save up money for a home and that although she was lonely she was pretty sure this was the right thing to do. She says: *The thing he taught me in our short time together was that any hope ought to be accompanied by action.*

This one causes silence. Maybe because it's good to think of Ben quietly changing a life, even at the last minute; and maybe also because everyone is worried about this talkative waitress who's very pregnant and now broke but kind enough to want to attend the funeral of a stranger.

That's when Renny stands up, a letter in her hand, and she says, *I think I'll let Ben speak for Ben.*

She clears her throat, holds the paper in her windblown red hands, and starts reading. *Dear Renny. If you're reading this, I'm dead. I have just been diagnosed with dementia, probably Alzheimer's. You just took me to the doctor last week.*

At that Carolyn lets out a yelp and Billy jumps a little in his seat and there is a collective surprise that floats in the air. No one knew of any letter. Renny shoots everyone an irritated look. When everyone calms down, she continues. *Renny, I am asking Eddie to keep this letter and give it to you when I die. I want to write it while my brain is still good. I'll probably forget I even wrote it someday.*

When Rachel died and we moved to separate ends of the ranch, well, maybe that's something we had to do. But as time went on, I was able to let go of the things that hurt. And instead I saw more and more of the strength and energy. In you, I mean. And I was just working myself up to ask if we could be together again—together in the same house, in the same marriage—when I started getting confused. Writing things on paper. And you moved me right back into the farmhouse, in your no-nonsense way, but I wish I had the courage to ask you if you wanted me. If you were still in love.

Here Renny pauses and looks straight out at us and says, in a quiet voice none of us have ever heard her use, *I was.* She says it twice more. *I was, I was.*

Renny squints, glances at the sky, which has moved from predusk to twilight to nearly dark. She stops and digs out a flashlight from her jacket, and reads the rest by a little circle of bobbing light. She reads: *I don't want to die, Renny. It doesn't feel right. Maybe it never does. But it feels like too many good years were ahead of me. I feel regret. Sure, I'd love to be young and strong again—wouldn't we all?—but that defies nature. I mean a different kind of regret. I accept my age, and I accept the facts of my life, maybe even I accept this disease. It's just that I'm not ready to go. I still want days to walk the farm and see the willows and visit with the grandkids. Play bridge with Eddie and irrigate with Carolyn. Bicker with you. It wasn't true that I wasn't interested in people. I was. I tried to take care of the land, which was my way of taking care of my family. I could have communicated it a little more, and asked you to do the same.*

Which is to say: I'm just not ready. But if you're reading this, I'm gone.

I loved that we had a life together on Hell's Bottom Ranch, and I love the stories that took place there. All except the story of Rachel, which was a sad one, too sad to bear. But the rest were good and beautiful. I love that we had a history together.

But I want to go out knowing who I am. That, I am sure you can understand. Please bury me by the willows. Maybe I'll be lucky enough to have the bald eagle or the owls watching.

At this, most people turn, but the bald eagle is not on its usual perch by the river. And anyway, it's getting too dark to differentiate between sticks and shadows. We scan the twilight sky, which is black-blue, but there are no birds anywhere. Among the murmurs and the sniffles, Satchmo looks up too and barks, just one single bark, which makes everyone laugh. The fire is crackling, and someone up front gets up to add a log.

Renny stands there, watching the sky with the rest of us. Then she shakes herself, like a dog getting up from sleep, and says: *Well, let's keep this short. Nothing worse than keeping people longer than they need to be kept. It's getting cold and dark. Anyone else?*

For a moment there is silence, and then in the fraction of a second before people start to move, before the gravediggers lower the coffin, before Ben goes into the ground, I stand up.

★

Tell you what I'm gonna do, see.

I often hear myself saying it, even now.

I say it to the river, I say it to the water that designs its own path as it spreads across the fields. I say it to water snaking down the irrigation ditch for the first time, and spreading across the field right as the sun is setting and hitting it just right, making it look like a sparkling sea. I say it to the beautiful earth, to the beautiful moon. I say it because to me, he was like a blue star, the kind that dies in the most spectacular of ways. Not, like the others, by shrinking up. But by exploding.

★

Stories help us perceive and possess our lives. They help us see our lives and then fully embrace them. So, in that way, there comes an afternoon when I look outside, at the clouds that have boiled up over the mountains, at their release of the first spatters of rain. Because of the height of the clouds, and the way they've formed, and the thunder, and the sudden energy in the air, I know that this will be the first real thunderstorm of spring.

In honor of Ben, I sit down in his old chair on the porch, next to the cowboy boots and muddy work boots and bailing strings. I look out the window and watch. This part of the story feels like it is narrated by the universe itself. The universe that's been watching us and this particular unfolding of a life and of a death. In certain rare moments of time, it all blends into one pure moment. Earth and sky and soul, all these become a remembering room. In that moment, here's what I notice: The felting beat of raindrops. How each individual drop hits the aspen tree leaves just outside the window. Each little leaf moves with the water, a drop here, a drop there. Some of the raindrops roll off the aspen leaf backwards, and others pool right in the center. It looks like the tree is conducting a symphony. A little jazz. One ping there, one plunk there. And here comes the onslaught, the plunks of water speeding up their tune. The green leaves comply, moving here and there, such a small motion, but somehow larger and larger as the whole tree comes to life. I can see Ben's mind, how it tumbled through memory. How our own brains do that, pinging with life when each new memory hits, a river of channels sparking into movement. Melting and freezing and flowing. I know that Ben used to sit here, in the same spot, and I understand that he would sometimes watch these first aspen leaves and spring rain, and that he would consider how the universe itself holds all this motion inside the stars, even as they are turning blue.

ACKNOWLEDGMENTS

To Jody Klein and Dan Smetanka: for believing.

To the Ucross Foundation, Earthskin Muriwai, and Playa: for time and space.

To Kent Haruf, Rick Bass, Laura Resau, Laura Hendrie, Dana Masden, Carrie Visintainer, Karye Cattrell, Janet Freeman, BK Loren, and Molly Reid: for your writing, careful reading, and writerly advice.

To James Pritchett, Morgan Smith, Todd Mitchell, Jim Davidson, Sharon Dynak, Andy Dean, Jim Brinks, Mary Dean, Kurt Gutjahr, Debbie Hayhow, Mary Lea Dodd, Gary Kraft, Debbie Berne, and the Alzheimer's Association in Fort Collins: for advice on particulars and friendship in general.

To Jake Pritchett, Ellie Pritchett, James Brinks, and Rose Brinks: for moments of grace.